Carol Arens delights in tossing fictional characters into hot water, watching them steam, and then giving them a happily-ever-after. When she's not writing she enjoys spending time with her family, beach-camping or lounging about in a mountain cabin. At home, she enjoys playing with her grandchildren and gardening. During rare spare moments you will find her snuggled up with a good book. Carol enjoys hearing from readers at carolarens@yahoo.com or on Facebook.

TO WED A WALLFLOWER

Carol Arens

MILLS & BOON

First published in Great Britain 2021
by Mills & Boon, an imprint of HarperCollins*Publishers* Ltd,
1 London Bridge Street, London, SE1 9GF

www.harpercollins.co.uk

HarperCollins*Publishers*
1st Floor, Watermarque Building,
Ringsend Road, Dublin 4, Ireland

Large Print edition 2021

To Wed a Wallflower © 2021 Carol Arens

ISBN: 978-0-263-28947-3

06/21

Printed and bound in Great Britain
by CPI Group (UK) Ltd, Croydon, CR0 4YY

For Claire Elizabeth De Cuir,
my sweet and witty granddaughter.
Your laughter sweetens our lives.

Chapter One

June 10th, 1890
—the writing desk in the library at Cliverton

Violet, my dearest and oldest friend,
But of course what else could you be, given
I've been witness to your increasing wrin-
kles over the years? I have bounded from
my bed to write to you about what has been
revealed to me.

I trust you will understand that 'bounded'
is merely an expression of my emotional
state...but I have had a dream. In it was re-
vealed that my niece will marry your son.

Not my niece Cornelia, you understand.
She was successfully wed last week. Nor is it
Felicia. As you may have heard she became
Viscountess Scarsfeld this Christmas past.

It is my sweet Ginny of whom I dreamed.

The poor girl is as shy as a mouse and I fear that without our guidance she will moulder away on the shelf. It has been many years since you have seen her, but be assured the Good Lord did not mean for this girl to moulder.

Your Phillip is out of mourning now, is he not? Surely he will be looking for a bride. He could not choose better than my Ginny.

I propose we encourage them, so to speak, towards that happy end.

I look forward to hearing your thoughts on the matter, sooner rather than later.
Your dearest and oldest friend,
Adelia

June 15th, 1890
—the writing desk in the library at Hawkwood

Adelia, my dearest and quite oldest friend,
Indeed, you could be nothing else given I have been witness to your ever-thickening waistline over the years...

A dream, you say? Involving my son and your niece? I can only assume this was no typical nightly fancy, since you hoisted your bones out of bed in the middle of the night to inform me of it.

As it turns out, I am concerned about poor Phillip. It is distressing that he has little interest in providing Hawkwood with a new countess. I do recall how sweet your niece was and as lovely as a rosebud, for all that she was only a wisp of a girl when I last saw her. Poor thing was distressed because she had got lost, as I recall.

Who are we to say she will not be the very one to give poor Phillip's heart a jolt? But you are certain it is Phillip you saw and not William? I do have two sons, after all.

It would not do if it was my younger son you dreamed of. The boy is a charming rascal and has no trouble turning the ladies' heads. It is poor, grieving Phillip we must help.

I have pressed him on the subject of marriage and he is quite sore of it by now. I must change my tactic, I think.

I shall schedule a country house visit here at Hawkwood, where Phillip and Ginny can be often in each other's company and we will not be detected as meddlers. As you might recall, Ullswater is particularly lovely in July.

Since you are not here with me to answer yea or nay, I will carry on with the scheme as if you were.

Cheers to our venture, my very dearest and by far my oldest friend.
In haste,
Violet

June 16th, 1890

Ginny loved her Aunt Adelia. Truly, she did.

The proof of it lay in the fact that she had accompanied her aunt on a score of social events both day and night. Having lived many years in the country, her aunt, the Marchioness of Montblue, was overjoyed to be back in London.

Yesterday they had attended tea at Lady Smyth's. Every day there were social calls to be paid to Auntie's many friends whom she had not seen in nearly a year. There had been a musical at the home of…who was it? Since her aunt had arrived to attend Cornelia's wedding, Ginny had been to so many places they blurred in her memory.

Last night they had attended the opera, which

was not truly awful. But tonight, here they were at a ball and it was awful.

Standing in the shadow of a large potted plant near the open ballroom doors, she peered through a smudge on the lenses of her black-rimmed spectacles. The glasses were annoying, but they did serve their purpose...once in a while.

Couples swirled past only yards from her inadequate hiding place. A swish of silk and satin whispered when they whisked by. Colours mingled in all the hues of a summer garden.

She adored dancing...as long as she was watching it and not attempting the steps. Sadly, she had no gift for it, only a longing.

If only she were more like her sister. Felicia could not sing, but she loved doing it and so she did. If anyone cast her an odd look, she never seemed troubled by it.

Oh, how Ginny wished she could feel the same. But being the centre of attention made her palms sweat and her heart race.

Standing here in deep shadow, feeling the brush of the ribbon on her dance card tickling her wrist, she was perfectly content to play the wallflower. Of course she was.

It was Aunt Adelia who was not content with it. Oh, she gossiped and laughed with the other matrons, but every now and then her gaze shifted to Ginny, which only went to confirm that even a large plant did very little to conceal her. It could not be long before Auntie, in a flourish of bright orchid satin, came to drag her into the light.

Oh, hang it! In the exact instant a young man detached himself from his group of fellows and walked towards her, Aunt Adelia swivelled her attention back to her friends.

Ginny had noticed him at various times during the evening because how could she not? He was exceptionally handsome while swaggering about and showering all the young ladies with his charm.

And now he was striding forward to rain it upon her. What was she to say to this paradigm of what a gentleman should be?

Nothing, that was what. Her thoughts and her voice would desert her. She would appear a perfect ninny. She could make a dash for the garden door, but that would make her look more of a ninny.

On he came, his smile and his eyes alight. Her palms grew damp while she wondered how she would carry on a conversation with this greatly sought-after gentleman. He was heir to a dukedom if she recalled correctly. Which she did since, although she could not dance, she was adept at recalling things.

'Good evening, Lady Virginia.' His eyes settled upon her, his smile lifting into place. 'I trust you are enjoying the evening?'

From the corner of her eye she noticed a freshly debuted young lady looking her way, her brows pressed in a worried frown. No doubt she longed to be standing in Ginny's place. Wouldn't the girl be surprised to know that Ginny would rather be anywhere else but here, trying to make polite conversation with Lord Hampton.

She could only imagine that after a bit of awkward conversation he would ask to be added to her dance card.

'Yes.' Even that one word felt thick. Why was it that speaking to a gentleman made her so self-conscious? Ladies were supposed to be gracious and witty. 'Quite.'

'May I point out,' he pointed out, the corner of his mouth quirking in a flirtatious flash, 'this gathering is greatly enhanced by your lovely presence?'

This would be the moment for a coquettish laugh. In all likelihood, if she attempted such a thing it would emerge as a croak. Instead she adjusted the ugly black glasses on her nose and remained silent.

Which was probably the most foolish thing she could do. Her cousin Peter, who had been her guardian since her parents' death, had often told her she could have her pick of gentlemen. All she needed to do was choose one and then encourage him just a little.

This was easy for Peter to say—he was a man and confident in everything he did.

For Ginny to encourage a gentleman, even one reputed to be as fine as Lord Hampton, was a trial.

She ought to make an effort, if not with him then with someone because she really did wish to have a husband and children. The idea of becoming a spinster was not a pleasant one, the very thought of it made her feel lonely.

Just because she was shy did not mean she did not enjoy the company of other people. She did… truly. And now that her sisters were married and no longer living at Cliverton, it only confirmed that a solitary existence was not something she desired.

'Lady Virginia, is there a spot on your dance card that I may have the honour of filling?'

Why could he not have asked for a trip to the buffet or the punch bowl? She might have managed that.

She opened her dance card, pretended to look it over. She glanced at the hopeful smile on the handsome heir to a dukedom's face. She tried to return the gesture, to answer, 'Yes, how lovely. My next dance is free.'

Sadly, what came out of her mouth was, 'Oh, thank you, my lord, but my dance card is full.'

It was…with names she had written in herself. She showed it too quickly for him to recognise that the names did not match a single fellow in attendance.

'Perhaps I will be luckier the next time we meet,' he said and then, with a smile that was not in the least resentful, he turned and approached another lady.

No doubt the next time they met he would be betrothed to a very happy woman.

Oh, hang it, but she disliked this trait of her

personality. It prevented her from truly partaking in the joy life had to offer.

Not only that, while she had avoided the humiliation of having to dance in front of people, within the hour Lord Hampton was going to discover her to be a liar.

He could hardly fail to notice that, despite all the names on her dance card, she was not dancing.

So far he had not, but that did not keep her from feeling half-nauseous over her cowardly and dishonest behaviour.

She could feign illness or injury and go home to avoid the questioning glance the man was bound to cast at her.

Indeed, she could do that, but Aunt Adelia was having such a grand time, it would be heartless to drag her away.

As if her aunt had read her thoughts, she left the ladies she was conversing with and made her way to Ginny's spot beside the plant.

'Oh, my dear!' Her expression glowed with expectation. 'I can only surmise that you have added Lord Hampton's name to your dance card. What a coup, Ginny!'

'I would have, of course, but my card is full.'

'Full? And yet here you stand rooted to the floor as securely as this palm is rooted to its pot.' Before Ginny could snatch it out of sight, Aunt Adelia snagged her dance card, opening it. 'Ginny Penneyjons, you made these names up! Really...please point out where Long John Silver is waiting for his dance. And of all the bad luck, I just saw King Arthur bidding our hostess farewell.'

'I do not wish to dance. I would look all elbows and knees. I might step on my partner's foot or stumble headlong against him.'

'Ginny, do you not wish to marry?'

'Of course I do, but—'

'You are by far the prettiest girl here. All you needed to do is encourage Lord Hampton and he would have been yours.'

'I'm not one to encourage strangers. I'm simply not.'

'But you must, otherwise no one will ever be more than a stranger to you. How can I possibly return home, thinking of you mouldering away at Cliverton?'

'I will not moulder, I will...' What she would do, she was not certain, but moulder? Certainly not! 'Perform works of charity.'

'Any lady of position will do the same, married or not. If you do not wish to return each day from your good works to a home occupied only by your staff, you must put more effort into securing a future which involves a family of your own.'

Aunt Adelia was correct. There was not a thing she could say to refute it so she remained silent.

'Well, you need not fear, my dear. I am here to set your future to rights as your mother would have me do.' Aunt Adelia let the dance card fall from her fingers with a quiet laugh. 'Rest assured we will find you a man more satisfying than Robin Hood.'

William Talton heard hoofbeats pounding the dirt path behind him. His horse held the lead, but the distance was growing shorter.

If he glanced to the right, he would see the blue water of Lake Ullswater flashing among the trees that grew near the shoreline of the estate.

He would not glance, not if the distraction caused him to give up even a foot of his lead. His brother Phillip was too fine a horseman to give him that advantage.

Looking at the lake was something he could

do from his chamber window, winning this race was not.

With a grin he sucked in a lungful of air, tasted the fresh scents of the last days of spring. It felt as though he was flying over the ground. A breeze lifted his hair and cooled the sweat on his neck.

Today he had every intention of besting his brother.

It had been a long hard year with the household in mourning for Phillip's young wife, but now the time for giving deference to his brother's grief was at an end.

A month or two ago he would have held back, let Phillip win the race in the hope that a victory would rally his brother's spirits.

Not now, though. It was time for Phillip to rejoin society. And if that meant him finally losing a race, so be it.

In truth, William enjoyed winning. Victory truly was sweet. As soon as his horse galloped across the finish line, marked by a tree half-burned by a lightning strike, he would let out a triumphant shout…the one he had been withholding during his brother's period of mourning.

The time had come for Phillip to step out of

the gloom which had both comforted and tormented him.

He loved his older brother far too much to hand him another unearned victory.

This certainly made William sound noble… as if he had behaved like some sainted, long-suffering hero when the truth of it was, beating Phillip would be like…

Wait! Those hoofbeats were closer than they ought to be.

The half-blackened tree was still twenty yards off and he could hear the panting breaths of the pursuing horse.

Looked as if his brother was racing out of the gloom all on his own. William would have to fight hard to win this competition.

From the corner of his eye he spotted movement. The shadow of a horse's nose stretched long on the path. Inch by inch it gained ground until he saw the nose of the beast and not just the shadow.

A dark blur against green foliage whizzed past. The race was finished.

'I win!' William shouted.

'You lose!' Phillip yelled simultaneously.

Phillip slowed his mount, let it prance about in

a bit of a victory circle, then slid out of the saddle. Grinning, he stroked his horse's strong neck.

'You are very cocky for a loser, Phillip.' William dismounted, then gave his brother's shoulder a companionable squeeze.

Phillip's brown eyes narrowed. He shook his head, clearing his brow of the damp strands of dark hair sticking to it.

His brother's dark looks were a contrast to William's fairer ones. Were it not for Mother's vow that they did, one might doubt they shared a father. One only needed to look at them side by side, she'd always insisted, to see they were nearly twins, save that one of them was sunshine and one was moon glow. One was mischief and one was obedience…and both of those traits reflected their dearly departed sire.

It did not take a great deal of reflection to know that Phillip was the obedient, responsible child. It was a lucky thing he was born first since he was far better suited to being a Hawkwood than William was.

For all that they were so different, he and his brother were close friends and brothers all at once.

'You only imagine you won. It is clear as day

that my horse is faster and I am the better rider. I did come from behind, after all. My victory would have been obvious had the tree been another ten yards off.'

'Better look up, big Brother. There is nothing clear about this day. It will be raining within the hour. And even had the finish line been further off, my horse was about to make a final sprint.'

William led his horse to the water's edge to let it have a short drink.

Phillip and his mount joined him at the shoreline.

Across the lake, the *Raven* sleekly cut the water, her decks filled with tourists who gazed at the shore, no doubt in awe of the beauty of water and land.

Ullswater was reported to be the most beautiful body of water in the Lake District. Not a day passed that he did not give thanks for being born and raised here.

'Did you know that Mother is planning to host a house party?' Phillip grumbled.

'She mentioned it. I think it is a good idea.'

'You would think so.' Although his brother was not looking at him, William sensed his frown. 'It's not you whom Mother is trying to marry off.

She claims the party to be only a spot of summer fun. But I know better. She is keen for me to wed and give Hawkwood an heir.'

'Mother is not subtle, at times.'

Perhaps not, but it was true that, as a Hawkwood, Phillip was required by society's dictates to wed again and provide the required heir.

In a sense, he felt sorry for his brother having to live by society's expectations of him.

William was free to live as he pleased for the most part. Free to choose a wife if or when he elected to do so.

Just now it was the last thing he wanted. Witnessing Phillip's grief after losing Cora had been enough to make him think better of making such a commitment. It wasn't only Cora's death, but his father's, too. The grim reaper wielded a cruel fist and William intended to avoid the blow in as much as he could.

'You would enjoy a house party, I imagine,' Phillip grumbled. 'Mother will invite eligible young ladies from far and wide…and their mothers.'

'I would not mind seeing the estate overrun by pretty faces.'

Phillip's snort said quite a lot.

'You will be free to make jolly with them, then bid them farewell. I will be expected to choose one and never bid her farewell.'

A shadow crossed his brother's eyes. Phillip had picked a lovely lady once and then bid her farewell in the harshest of ways.

'It's what you need, Phillip. Society's demands be hanged. You need a wife because it suits you to have one. I don't think you can be happy otherwise.'

'Maybe you are right. But how will I know which lady will suit? It was clear with Cora, we'd known each other all our lives. But the women Mother is inviting are strangers. For all that Mother calls it a summer fête, we know the ladies have only one thing in mind in coming here and it has nothing to do with my charming self.'

'You are charming when you give it half an effort.'

'It matters little whether I have the charm of a bear or a peacock and you know it. Either is acceptable when a young lady is in pursuit of social position.'

'You can't hold it against them. It is not as if they are free to choose a husband. They have been trained to wed a title as much as you have been to be that title.'

Wind blew in off the lake, fresh and cool. It was one of the scents of Hawkwood that William loved most so he lifted his nose to breathe it in.

He was more grateful to his brother than anyone knew for the efficient way he oversaw Hawkwood's finances. Phillip loved numbers and business so the estate always posted a good profit.

This left William free, along with the estate manager, to care for the day-to-day running of the estate. There was not a job in creation he would enjoy more.

'Well, I do not fault them, of course. It's just... Cora... I knew what it was like to love my wife. I would have that again, if I can.'

If anyone deserved to, it was Phillip.

Clouds pressing upon the tops of the fells crept darkly down towards the lake.

'We had better get the horses to the stables,' his brother pointed out.

Turning away from the lake, they walked the path they had just raced along.

'I don't know how I would recognise her, the woman I might love,' Phillip mumbled. 'Not through all the posturing and competition to win Hawkwood. How will I know who is genuine?'

'I will recognise her for you.'

His brother laughed quietly under his breath while shaking his head.

'How do you propose to do that?'

'The ladies will not be competing for me…at least not for the same reason they will be competing for you.' Vain words? Completely, but he would utter them again if only to hear Phillip's snort of amusement. It was far too long since he had heard such a noise spout from his brother.

Rain began to splat gently on trees growing alongside the path, but he and Phillip continued at a relaxed pace.

Phillip—the Phillip he had been before they lost Cora—was coming back to him…to life, really…and William had no wish to end the moment.

'What I mean is that I will see things in them that they will not reveal to you.'

'Shall I give you my desired list of qualities in a lady so you may sift them out?' The sarcasm in his brother's voice did not altogether disguise his desire for help.

'No need, I know it well enough.'

Again, an expression darkened Phillip's eyes… a shadow, or a glance at the past, perhaps. To William's relief it vanished before it could drag him backwards into grief.

'I'm fascinated to find who you come up with, little Brother.'

So was he. He had never taken on a role of matchmaker before.

Also, it was going to be an interesting thing to see which ladies Mother deemed acceptable as opposed to the ones that William thought were.

Even more interesting would be to discover whether his brother formed an attachment to any lady in attendance.

William was not certain it was possible to make a love match so quickly. In his opinion, love needed longer than a house party to steal one's heart. Water in a pot was a good example— it did not boil the instant it was put to flame.

But he was no expert at love given that his pot had never heated past simmer.

Maybe he was wrong…he knew first-hand that puppy love could happen in an instant so perhaps the adult form of it could as well.

What he did know was that it would be an interesting experience, helping Phillip sort out the intentions of the ladies vying for him.

Honestly, he could not recall looking forward to a house party more than this one.

Chapter Two

It was a rare afternoon.

Not, Ginny thought, rare as in the sunny warmth of the day—June in London was one of her favourite months—but rare in that Aunt Adelia had no social excursions planned.

The afternoon was blissfully and wonderfully free. With all the engagements of late, Ginny had neglected writing in her journal. She well and truly missed it.

With Aunt Adelia resting and the house quiet, she tucked a quilt under her arm, gathered her writing supplies into a basket, then went to the garden.

She spread the quilt in the dappled shade of a tree. Sitting down and leaning back against the trunk, she exhaled a grateful sigh. With her eyes closed, she saw shifting patterns of light against her lids. She looked past them searching for…

'Oh, there you are,' she murmured.

The lady of Ginny's own fiction, Justina Admirable, stood before her, hands curled on hips while waiting impatiently for her adventure to be put to pen and ink.

'And who would you like to caper with today? Of course, Lord Handsome and Bold it is. Yes, believe me, I know, it has been days since you have been with him.'

Ginny lifted her pen and with a smile put the tip on the paper. Today she would give her characters a grand adventure.

'A storm broke over the moor, stabbing the turf with great crashes of lightning.' Ginny shivered because she, herself, feared storms. 'Hair tossed by the wind and her cape being lashed about her body, Justina pushed boldly through the elements. No matter the cost to her safety, she must get to the ball at Legend House. The man she loved was under a spell and was about to fall into the clutches of a seductress. This was a catastrophe not to be borne!'

Her pen fairly flew across the paper. Justina charged into the ballroom to find her hero, the broad-shouldered and blue-eyed Lord Handsome and Bold—Ginny could name him that since not a soul in creation would ever read this—nearly impaled on the fortune hunter's talons.

What the seductress did not realise was that Justina's charm was enough to yank any man back from the brink of insanity. Especially this one who, when in his right mind, was completely devoted to her.

'Unhand my paramour, you trollop,' Ginny muttered while scratching pen across paper. The villainess would not have him this day!

Oh, Justine was bold. Assertive and charming, Ginny's pen-and-ink self was everything that she was not. The clever lady had finagled herself out of many difficulties over the years in which Ginny had been crafting stories.

'Are you writing to anyone I know, my dear?'

Ginny started, nearly dropping her pen.

If this was not one of the most embarrassing moments of her life, she did not know what was. Her most guarded secret...her fantasy self... exposed!

'Naturally not... I was just writing a bit of... of poetry.'

Aunt Adelia's half-sly smile plumped her cheeks, turning them pink. She tapped her chin with one finger. 'It sounds delightfully sordid, although it does not rhyme.'

'I was just about to add...' What on earth rhymed with trollop? '"Else I shall pummel with a wallop."'

'Oh, that is lovely.' There was a bench close to the blanket so her aunt spread her colourful skirts and sat upon it. 'May I ask you something, Ginny?'

'Of course, Auntie.' She shut her writing tablet, hoping the ink would not smear, also hoping the question had nothing to do with her private missive.

'I wonder, isn't it easier for you to write the sonnet with your glasses on? I cannot imagine they do much good lying beside your knee as they are.'

Why must her aunt be so perceptive? Were not older ladies supposed to be delightfully forgetful?

'Oddly, I tend to see better without them when I write.' She saw better without them for everything, but she was not about to admit that.

She reached for the glasses, but Aunt Adelia reached quicker. Her aunt was as agile as she was perceptive.

Holding them up to the light, she turned them this way and that. She plonked them on her nose.

Oh, but those truly were ugly glasses! What an excellent purchase they had been.

'Fakes.' Aunt Adelia blinked through the big black frames. 'And if you believe your beauty is diminished because of them you are mistaken.'

Of course it was diminished…it had to be!

Having a pretty face had been a bother all her life. Because she was said to resemble 'an angel touching the earth'—some smitten fellow had actually pronounced that sentiment aloud—people tended to stare at her.

Ever since she could remember, she had hated being stared at. Adults had cooed over her, announced to one and all that she was the prettiest child they had ever seen. Really, did they never notice how saying such a thing in front of other children made them envious…made them resent her?

It was better to cling to Mother's skirts and hide. And so she had. Even at two years old, she found the folds of Mother's dress to be a great comfort.

The glasses were a poor replacement, but they did work, usually.

Her aunt plucked the glasses off and set them back where they were. 'If you want to know the truth, these glasses, as unattractive as they are, add a dash of mystery to your beauty.'

Certainly not! Please let it not be true that she suffered the weight on her face for no reason whatsoever!

Oh, hang it! If her aunt was correct, and Ginny was not convinced that she was, wearing the beastly things had done her effort to be ignored more harm than good.

'Come up here and sit beside me, my dear.' Aunt Adelia patted the bench so Ginny rose and sat next to her. At once she was immersed in the fragrance of roses.

There had always been something comforting about Aunt Adelia's scent.

Her aunt was always with the family in times of crisis. Once when Father was deathly ill and again when Peter arrived at Cliverton, a weeping orphan. When the entire household came down with influenza, Auntie had been there to nurse them through it. Mama often told of how Ginny was a breech birth and that both of them would certainly have died had Aunt Adelia not sat beside her, gripping her hand and demanding that she not give up, but push through the fear and the pain. Aunt Adelia would accept no other outcome.

Mostly, what Ginny would never forget was the scent of roses and Aunt Adelia's arms wrapped about her when she suddenly became an orphan. On her darkest day, her aunt had held her fast.

'Why do you hide? Do you not wish to marry some fine gentleman and fall in love with him? Surely you want what your sisters have?'

Naturally, most women did.

What she ought to do was take a lesson from her sister Felicia. When Lord Scarsfeld requested to wed one of the Penneyjons girls, her sister had boldly gone forth to meet the man while Ginny had chosen to stay home where life was safe and predictable. Now her sister was quite happy as Lady Scarsfeld.

In the end it was for the best that it was Felicia to have gone and not Ginny. But still, what might have happened if she had her sister's courage?

It was what she wanted. But when she imagined doing what her sister had done…well, it made her feel half sick.

Indeed, sick with dread…also sick with disgust at herself for being timorous.

She needed to face the fact that by being so bashful, she was missing opportunities to meet some very decent gentlemen.

Why was it that she failed to learn the lesson of her sister's boldness?

She did not honestly believe she was a coward at heart. If only she could release Justina Admirable from the pages of her journal.

'I do want that…just not what comes before… socialising and speaking to strangers. I get so tied up with nerves I do not know what to say to make charming conversation. If only I could skip that part and go straight to being in love.'

'Oh, but the getting to know him part is quite delicious! Trust me, Ginny, you would not want to miss it.'

That was easy for her aunt to say, she could speak to anyone about anything and enjoy doing it.

'You always have been a shy little flower.' Auntie patted her cheek, smiling as pictures from the past seemed to bloom in her mind. 'You would screech and carry on, clinging desperately to your mother if a stranger but said hello. You were so attached to her. Do you know, every once in a while when you were a tot, I worried you'd gone missing and then I would see a particular smile light your mother's face. It was one she had for you alone, I'll never forget it. Then your mother would sweep aside her skirt and there you would be, laughing at the great joke you'd played on your auntie.'

'I remember. The ivory skirt with the pink flowers was my favourite. The fabric was sheer and I could see you looking for me. You looked so concerned until you caught Mama's eye.'

Aunt Adelia glanced at the sky, blinking for a moment.

'Yes, indeed... I miss her dreadfully.'

An icy street and a carriage skidding out of control...life as they had all known it vanished in that instant... Mama, Ginny's rock, her security...gone.

Even though it was more than ten years ago, the memory of that night swelled a lump in her throat.

'But here we find ourselves, left behind to make the best of our world until we see them again. It is what they wish us to do, don't you agree?'

'I do.' And she did. 'But sometimes the wait seems a very long one.'

'Which is why we must fill up the time with things which will honour their memory, such as meeting new people, finding new love. Marrying and adding babies to the family. Can you imagine how empty life would be if we did not?'

'You seem fulfilled, Auntie, and you did not remarry after Uncle Alfred died.'

'The secret to it is waking each morning and looking for the joy in the day rather than the trouble. And I do enjoy my friendships. Besides, there is nothing to say that I will not marry again. There's still a bit of life beating in this old bosom.'

'I only wish I had half of it.'

'But of course you do. You are as frisky and spirited as the next young lady. It is my belief that with a bit of practice that young lady will be released upon society.'

What did she mean? 'Practice?'

'I understand why you hold yourself back. Of course it is understandable. In your grief you shrank in upon yourself…your tendency to be bashful became exaggerated. How long have you been hiding behind those glasses, my dear?'

'Since I debuted and attracted the attention of every gentleman in need of a wife.'

'But it is how society works, the purpose of coming out.' Aunt Adelia brushed a stray wisp of hair behind Ginny's ear...her touch an echo of Mama's. 'It is time to put the fear behind you. Nothing would please your parents more than to see you stepping out, finding happiness with a fellow of your own.'

It was the truth. She ought to have outgrown being a timid little girl long ago.

In the company of those she loved, she was frisky and spirited. At the true heart of herself, it was who she was. Unfortunately, to everyone else she was a mouse...a pretty one, yes, but a rodent just the same.

She could only recall one person outside her family who she had ever allowed to see her...to look inside and see the Ginny Penneyjons who was as brave and fun as anyone else.

She had spent only a day with that boy. It was shortly after her mother died, but she had never forgotten him...as Lord Handsome and Bold attested to. Although she had not seen him since, she sometimes wondered what kind of man he had turned into. If the boy was any hint of it, he must have become someone wonderful and kind. She remembered that about him...he was kind and such fun!

In the privacy of her heart, she occasionally dreamed of what it would be like if she were to meet him again, but—

'We will begin practising speaking to strangers tomorrow. By the time we arrive at Hawkwood you will be at ease among company.'

'Hawkwood?'

Truly?

Her heart nearly tripped over itself.

'Of course, my dearest friend in all the world. You recall her, I'm sure. Violet Talton?—of course, you were but a child when you last saw her, so perhaps not. At any rate, she is having a country party. Her son is out of mourning and she hopes to reintroduce him to society...to find him a bride is what she really intends. We, my darling girl, will attend. I believe the pair of you will suit quite well. I've no doubt you will be the very young lady to capture his attention.'

But she could not possibly! Leave the safety of home and travel north? For all that she wished—

'I do not—'

Aunt Adelia waved away her half-hearted protest. Half-hearted because Ginny had been too fearful to travel north once before.

She must remember the lesson to be learned, how avoiding risk might be a huge mistake.

Avoiding risk in this instance might be an even greater folly.

Lady Talton had two sons.

The younger of them was known to Ginny as Lord Handsome and Bold.

'Isn't it a pity Peter was not able to travel to Ullswater with us? But estate business must be attended to.'

Aunt Adelia's smile, her speculative gaze and the way her finger tapped her chin gave her true feelings away.

Oh, indeed, her aunt was glad not to have Peter underfoot where he might object to Ginny...his cousin, his ward, and his responsibility...purposefully engaging the attention of strangers... of gentleman Peter was not already acquainted with.

Peter had not been fond of the idea of them travelling alone but he could hardly object since Aunt Adelia was an appropriate chaperon.

Now, here they were, listening to the shriek of

the train whistle, feeling the vibration of metal wheels creeping along steel tracks as the train pulled away from the station.

The sound made her nerves jump, but not the sound really, just that it indicated the time had come for her to be tested.

Over the course of the past three weeks, Ginny had been instructed on how to appear self-possessed. Or if not that, to at least not stare at the floor when a gentleman approached.

Experience had taught her that it would not be long before she caught the attention of some fellow and the results of Auntie's instruction would be known as a success or a failure.

Chin up, she reminded herself. Not an easy feat to maintain even had her glasses been on her nose…but with them tucked away in her luggage…well?

Her heart fluttered nervously in anticipation of an inevitable encounter. Even though she had practised smiling and conversing for hour upon hour, her gentleman had been Aunt Adelia.

Engaging in vivacious discourse with a human male was bound to prove more daunting.

However, her aunt was not wrong in attempting to teach her to become socially at ease. If she ever hoped to have a life not dependent upon Peter's charity, a home and a family of her own to love, she would need to emerge from her shell.

Her mind drifted for a moment, wondering how different Lord Handsome and Bold was from the man she had written him to be. Really, it was a sixteen-year-old boy she remembered... but he had been handsome and bold.

Suddenly, Aunt Adelia kicked her boot under the joined billow of their travelling gowns.

Ginny blinked back to the here and now to find a man smiling at her, apparently being introduced by Aunt Adelia.

Had he just muttered that it was a pleasure to meet her? Coming to awareness midway into the introduction, she was not certain. Well, hopefully so since she was about to respond in kind.

'How very lovely it is to meet you, as well, my lord.' Smile...she should smile and say something coquettish. 'I trust you are having a fine morning. Isn't this the most elegant railway car? It is nearly as if we are...well, as if we are at a grand gala before we reach the gala.'

This was horrid, her face must be blushing a thousand and one shades of red.

'Yes, well, as Lord Bixby was just telling us, he is on his way to his mother's sickbed.' Aunt Adelia gave the gentleman a fetching smile. 'I hope you will forgive my niece. She is under stress, I am afraid. She is deathly afraid of rail travel and the motion of the train must have disoriented her for a moment, is that not right, Virginia?'

Well, at least the man was smiling. She must not have offended him too greatly.

'I do beg your pardon, Lord Bixby. My attention truly had wandered. I will pray that you find your mother in recovering health.'

That was easily said because she meant it. As soon as he walked away she would offer up that prayer.

'Thank you, Lady Virginia. May I say how I appreciate your very caring words?'

She nodded. Aunt Adelia kicked her foot once again. Clearly, she was meant to carry on with the conversation.

With this venture in social grace taking such a dismal turn, Ginny could not find the courage to resume.

Luckily, her aunt suffered no such lapse. Aunt Adelia and Lord Bixby spent several moments speaking together as if they had not only just met.

When the gentleman went on his way her aunt gave her a bright smile.

'Well done, Ginny!'

'It was horribly done, as you well know.'

'In the beginning, yes, and that only because you were caught unaware. But you finished quite nicely.'

'Nicely? I looked a perfect fool.'

'I doubt if he cared greatly. I imagine it is not every day a man who...well, of his appearance shall we say...is shown kindness by a lady who looks like you do.'

'I have no idea what you mean...what of his appearance?'

'The pock marks on his face? Surely you must have noticed.'

'I was too busy feeling an idiot to notice anything but my own thoughtless words. I'm sure Lord Bixby was perfectly presentable even with it.'

Was it not interesting that even with what might be considered a disfigurement, he could carry on in a confident, affable manner. She had always felt that, in a sense, her beauty was disfigurement because she was judged by it the same as Lord Bixby must be. It was a rare person who did not look past her face to see the person inside.

Maybe this lesson was not such a failure. Indeed, she had much to learn from Lord Bixby.

'And now I will pray for his poor mother,' Ginny said, folding her hands and bowing her head.

'So shall I.'

After asking a blessing on Lady Bixby, Ginny kept her eyes closed. Anyone walking past would assume she was dozing.

Which was not so far from the truth since she was daydreaming…looking back on the time she had spent with not Phillip, but his younger brother, William. Although she had been but twelve years old, she recalled it vividly.

Ginny had lost her parents six months earlier. Lady Hawkwood had lost her husband, and William his father, at nearly the same time.

Adelia had decided there had been enough grieving even though the year of mourning was not up. She arranged to bring the families together for a weekend at her estate near Nottingham.

There had been a picnic with several people in attendance, even a bishop who was a friend of the Talton family had attended to offer what comfort he could.

There had been many children present, dashing about laughing and playing follow-the-leader. But Ginny sat under a tree, wanting to join in the fun, but too shy to make the move.

Then one of them, an older boy, turned from the others, stood quite still and looked at her. He smiled, then came and sat down beside her.

From the start she and William got along easily together. For some reason it did not seem to matter that he was sixteen years old to her twelve. Perhaps it had to do with their common grief...or their shared need to escape from it for an afternoon.

If she lived to be a grand old woman, she would not forget that, of everyone he might have chosen to sit beside to eat lunch, here he was with her.

And as unbelievable as it seemed, her tongue did not get tied up in her thoughts when she spoke to him.

Conversation was not strained. Indeed, not

once did she stumble over finding something clever to say. They both felt the ache of loss and that perhaps explained the easy manner between them, but that was not all of it.

He liked boat rides, so did she. She liked to run fast with her hair loose, he did as well. They both liked reading and sitting in quiet places listening to rain. And ducks—they were both mad about the funny feathered creatures.

So when he had glanced over at her with a wink and a nod towards a wooded area, she nodded back without hesitation.

Discreetly, he gathered food into a napkin and tucked it under his coat.

He grinned and they both stood up.

No one would have thought it amiss if they went for a walk together, but for some reason it seemed more fun to sneak away.

Running hard and laughing, they were completely breathless when they stopped to rest beside a stream.

'Do you think they noticed us sneak away?' he asked and winked at her.

'I'm certain they did, but dashing away was great fun anyway.'

She might be only twelve years old, but she

was a girl and so she could not help but notice that her friend William was handsome. That he had asked her, of all the children at the picnic, to sneak away with him was thrilling. It made her feel special.

He withdrew a berry tart from the napkin and offered it to her. When he set it in her open hand his knuckle brushed her palm.

Instantly, she was smitten with a fine and glorious crush.

An hour passed while they sat beside the stream. Even though her twelve-year-old heart tickled as fitfully as a butterfly, she was not nervous. Perhaps because despite him being her Galahad…her Lancelot…not once did he ever look at her as if she was merely a silly girl.

No, indeed. When a duck waddled awkwardly past with five ducklings trailing, then ruffled her feathers and squawked at one which lagged behind the rest, he laughed as heartily as she did. When the small creature began to toddle in the wrong direction, Will scooped it up.

By now he was that… Will, her friend, and dear enough to have a pet name.

He let her stroke the duckling for a moment

before he placed it in the water where it scurried after its family.

Another delightful hour passed while they sat beside the stream. She had a smear of berry tart on her nose and for some reason they both found it to be hilarious.

There had not been a time before, or after, in which she laughed so freely unless it was with a sister.

The strangest thing was, for all that she had just met him, Will felt nearly like family…but to be honest, laughing with her sisters never made her heart flutter.

It was the oddest sensation because although she understood their acquaintance was only a few hours old, it seemed they had been friends for ever.

Over the intervening years she had given a great deal of thought to it. She could only imagine the bond had to do with them both missing their parents so dreadfully. Grieving united them in a way that made their time together seem sweet, poignant.

Having such a grand time sitting beside the stream, neither of them noticed a storm coming upon them.

It took a great roll of thunder to make them aware of the change in the weather.

The manor house was a great way off, but as luck would have it, Will spotted a cave in a nearby hillside. He caught her hand and hurried her towards the shelter, from where they sat, side by side at the cave entrance, watching lightning jab the earth in electric explosions. Thunder boomed so close at hand she wondered if rocks would shake loose.

He must have felt her shiver.

'You scared?' he asked.

'No.' Of course she was, but she did want to look brave. 'Are you?'

He shook his head. His hair, still wet and glistening from the run to the cave, dripped water down his nose.

Of course he would not be frightened. He was a boy and no doubt used to playing in storms and caves.

'I just thought if you were...well, I'm here so you needn't be.'

And then the most wonderful thing happened. He took her hand and held it. The most handsome, the very boldest and kindest boy she had ever met vowed to protect her.

'Would you like to talk about your parents?' he asked.

For all that she did not wish to speak of them, to feel the lump in her throat that always swelled when she did…

'Yes…and you must tell me about your father.'

So they did. He told her his stories and she told him hers. They cried, of course, but they also held each other…and then they laughed. It was over nothing really, but when they were finished, they wiped their eyes.

Everything seemed better then, not just the storm, but with simply living and breathing and accepting that Mama and Father were in Heaven.

'I hope they aren't too worried about us,' she said, meaning the people they had dashed away from. Her parents would not be worried. Not if they were looking down and seeing her safe with William Talton.

'I do hope they don't come looking.' He nodded at her in the deepening gloom. She liked his dimples when he smiled.

'It might be dangerous.' She watched rain turning everything to mud. Perhaps they should not have dashed away.

'Could be, but that's not why I said it. I think

I don't want to be found just yet. I like spending time with you, Ginny.'

'I like spending time with you, too.' So easily stated, it was the truth. Nothing she was certain had ever been more natural to say. 'I don't mind if we remain until morning.'

'But we can't, you know that.' He squeezed her hand. 'We're young, but still, we would not want people to talk.'

'Oh, I hadn't thought.'

But she should have. At sixteen he would soon be making a turn towards becoming a man.

At twelve...well, she was not about to make a turn towards becoming a woman for all that her body was beginning to make subtle changes.

'As soon as it is safe, I will take you back.'

'I hope it is never safe, then.' Had she really uttered such a thing?

Indeed she had and she'd meant it.

Oh, my, but she had been so very young and innocent. No doubt as the years passed, he had quite forgotten that time in the cave.

She would be foolish to imagine he had not. Why, any man so handsome and wonderful was bound to be married by now, perhaps even the father of a child or two.

In the end the lightning had passed. Heavy rain turned into a gentle patter. They left the cave and made their way down to the manor house, led by a soft yellow glow of lamps in the windows.

When they reached a path leading to the front door, Will indicated that she should go on without him.

'Tell them we were separated and you do not know where I am.'

'But why?'

'A lady should not be alone with a gentleman. It is not proper and I would not bring disgrace upon you.'

'I'm not a lady, not yet.'

A funny expression crossed his face. 'But I'm close to being a gentleman…a few more years and I will be.'

And then the most amazing thing happened. He bent down and placed a quick kiss on her forehead. 'Some day, when you are grown, I'll find you and marry you.'

And then, just like that, he was gone.

She and her family departed for home the next morning. She had heard nothing from him or even about him during the intervening years.

Which was not to say she had not written

words about him…no, indeed, she had written thousands.

Did William Talton in the present day bear an ounce of resemblance to Lord Handsome and Bold? Probably not. Time changed everyone.

Her written words were a fantasy and nothing more. Perhaps she ought to have stopped writing them long ago. And yet there was a comfort to crafting stories. Artists crafted images out of paint. Ginny crafted them out of words.

She opened her eyes, watching the world rush past the train window.

Although it had not changed her all that much. At heart she was still a shy little mouse.

This was something she hoped very much to change. Under her aunt's tutelage, she was going to venture boldly into polite society. Life as she knew it was about to change.

Indeed, she would strive her hardest to make it so.

Left on her own, she might be content to find her joy writing childhood fantasy.

'What do you know about the Earl of Hawkwood, Auntie?' she asked, putting the past where it belonged. 'I know that we met one time, but I was only a little girl and to my mind he was one of the adults so I did not pay much attention to him.'

Her aunt turned to her with a great smile.

Really, Ginny ought to have asked about him before now. She had been so consumed with learning how to speak easily with him, she had given Phillip Talton, the man, little thought.

Not nearly as much as she had given his younger brother. A situation she must seek to change.

An extremely eligible earl was seeking a wife and Ginny was done with the spectre of spinsterhood.

People looked at spinsters with pity…pity that was not always kind. But, no…to avoid those stares was not the reason she was seeking marriage. She could avoid stares easily enough by hiding away as she had always done.

What she wanted, and wanted badly enough to venture forth on this trip with Auntie, was a man of her own to love. And his children. A family of her own to care for.

'But you would not remember him, naturally.' Aunt Adelia tapped her chin in thought. 'A twelve-year-old would have no more interest in a twenty-year-old than he would have in her. Of course, those eight years make no difference now.'

'I suppose what I would like to know is if you think we will suit each other? Will he make a good husband?'

'I know he will. I would not bring you to meet him if I did not think so. He was devoted to his late wife, so that is in his favour. Truly, my dear, Lord Hawkwood is quite a reliable and steady man.'

'There will be many ladies seeking to capture his affection...ladies younger and more vivacious than I am.'

'You make it sound as if you are in your dotage. Truly, Ginny, do you not know how beautiful you are? Phillip will see only you.'

And that was where the problem lay. She did know how pretty she was. Even when she was quite young her looks were remarked upon, the same as people were remarked upon for supposed flaws in their appearance.

No one saw who she really was. They fell in love with her face...not her heart or soul.

She could only hope Phillip Talton would be different.

Chapter Three

It was a fine afternoon so when William's mother made the unusual request for him to accompany the large, open-air carriage to Penrith and collect a few of her guests from the train station, William gladly consented.

Her party was to be a different sort of affair, Mother had explained. Informal, free of some of the stuffy restrictions of London society. Mother's country gathering was to be one in which gentleman and ladies might more easily enjoy one another's company.

More to the point, one in which Phillip's path to love might be unhampered. Since it was Mother's party, her rules would be observed.

William approved. Society's dictates could be stifling sometimes. Perhaps this gathering would be refreshing.

While picking up Mother's guests might appear to be doing her a favour, in truth, the favour was done to him.

A few moments to enjoy a bit of peace was what he needed.

The manor house buzzed with activity. He had seen it this way many times and knew the result of the work would be an event that appeared to come off with no effort at all.

Mother was an accomplished hostess and so he expected all would fall into place as she wished it to.

Every little detail from what food was served, what entertainment was offered, along with every piece of music to be played at the intimate ball, would happen as she planned it to.

His mother was a wonder of organisation.

It remained to be seen whether the purpose of the event, finding a new countess for Hawkwood, a wife for Phillip, would fall neatly into step with her plans.

William thought it might. His brother was ready to share his life, replace his loneliness with contentment. Given there would be a dozen eager ladies wanting the role of Countess of Hawkwood, he thought Mother would get her way in it.

He only hoped there would be a lady among them worthy of his brother's loyal heart.

When he had promised Phillip to help discover who among them would best suit, he had meant it.

To call the undertaking a burden would not be accurate. He greatly looked forward to meeting the ladies. Most of them were not from Ullswater because Mother wanted to present her son with women he was not already familiar with.

Yes, William did look forward to making their acquaintance, yet at the same time he was relieved it was not he who was required to pick a bride.

His life was ideal the way it was. What would be the point of risking his heart, possibly suffering the grief of loss, when he was content as he was?

He did admire Phillip for taking the risk again. But William wondered if it was even possible to make such a choice based upon a country party.

It might be if a man was not particular about the lady he chose to fill the role. But Phillip was particular. His brother knew what marriage could be and would not be happy with anything less than that.

If a lady did strike his brother's fancy all would be well and good, but if one did not? There was nothing to say this gathering would be Phillip's only opportunity, for all that Mother designed it to be successful.

Listening to the whistle of the train shrilly cutting through the tranquillity of the afternoon as it drew near the depot, he determined to do his utmost to sort out the genuine hearts from the scheming ones.

As weighty a task as it was, ferreting out which lady would make his brother happy did leave William feeling satisfied…in a helpful and novel way.

It was going to be a pleasant task, to be sure. He was glad to have gathered a few bunches of dog rose before leaving Hawkwood. The pretty pink blossoms were sure to make the ladies feel welcome.

Watching passengers disembark, William grinned. Of all the tasks his mother had assigned him in preparation for the house party, this one was the most pleasant. Meeting new people, welcoming them to Hawkwood, was always a pleasure.

Of the people stepping off the train, most were

tourists who had come to walk around the lake. It was a popular thing to do for the upper class. Others were probably here to take a cruise on the *Raven*. The boat was nearing the first anniversary of its launch and there was more interest in it than usual.

Tourists certainly had picked a fine day to visit. Bright, warm sunshine felt something like a caress. It was as if it relayed a blessing upon lake and fells from their Creator.

Shopkeepers would be pleased about so many folks coming to the town to spend their money. As late in the day as it was, they would likely be spending the night at the local inns.

Scanning the faces of people stepping on to the platform, he knew one to be on the watch for, his mother's friend, the Marchioness of Montblue. It had been a few years since he had seen her, but the lady was rather unforgettable. He had always thought Adelia Monroe to be a bit like champagne, having a bubbly spirit which could not be contained in a mere flute. Indeed, she spread effervescence upon anyone within her sphere.

The Marchioness was bringing a young lady with her, but Mother had not mentioned who she was. Adelia Monroe had three nieces, he recalled, two who were married. More than likely it was the youngest who was accompanying her, but was she of an age to marry already? In his mind he could only summon the image of a thin and pretty child. He also recalled spending one of the best days of his life in her company.

That had been a lifetime ago. He would be surprised if she remembered the day.

The other lady he was watching for was the Countess of Robinn. He had not met her before, but Mother thought she would be easy to spot because the Countess would be wearing red feathers in her hat…she always wore red feathers.

Ah, there she was, stepping off the train and on to the platform, crimson feathers bobbing merrily on her hat. Lady Robinn's steps were purposeful, her daughter's more hesitant while she glanced about wide-eyed. Her blinks of curiosity gave her away as being freshly debuted.

Striding forward, two bunches of flowers in hand, he introduced himself then escorted them to the carriage.

Returning to the platform, he instructed a porter to have their luggage delivered to Hawkwood. He felt Lady Della Starling's gaze settle between his shoulder blades, staring at his back while he walked back to the platform. If the girl was appraising him, she might turn out to be fickle… not at all the one for Phillip.

To be fair, though, it was early to form opinions, especially on one so newly released into society.

Ah, there was Adelia Monroe being helped down the steps by a man who appeared to be a fellow passenger. She had not changed in the years since he had last met her and he was glad to see she had not.

A younger lady stepped down after her, being aided by the same gentleman.

William could not see the young lady's face because she was looking down while the man spoke to her. Only a blind man would fail to notice she was uncomfortable with the fellow's attention…or adoration, it seemed.

William sensed her discomfort even with her face turned to him in profile.

Adelia Monroe chatted happily with the porter.

She would, of course. The Marchioness, he recalled, gathered friends as easily as some people gathered flowers. The fact that the fellow was not of her social standing made no difference to her apparent enjoyment of the conversation.

William hurried towards her, genuinely pleased to see her again.

'Lady Montblue.' Taking her soft hand, he returned her squeeze of greeting. 'It is good to see you again.'

'Oh, pish-posh! Lady Montblue? Your mother is my very dearest friend in the world. I will be crushed if you do not call me Aunt Adelia. You used to, you know.'

Yes, he did know, but it had been an awfully long time ago when he was but a boy.

'Welcome to Ullswater, Aunt Adelia. Mother is anxious to see you.'

'No more than I am to see her, my dear William.'

All at once the young lady looked up. She spun about, leaving the gentleman to converse with the back of her hat. The fellow was saying something about continuing their acquaintance.

She peered up at William from under her gaily flowered hat brim. Her eyes were the lavender-blue shade of a harebell blossom. There had only been one time in his life he had seen eyes that shade.

'Virginia, come and meet William Talton, the son of our hostess.'

The gentleman Virginia had been speaking with snapped his mouth closed. He had been neatly dismissed by the Marchioness and no mistake about it. Spinning about on his boot heel, he stomped off.

'Oh, but perhaps you will remember each other?' Aunt Adelia tapped her chin thoughtfully. 'But of course, you could not...not really. It was so long ago that you met and then only briefly.'

William could not imagine she would remember him because, indeed, it was years ago and they had been no more than children.

And Aunt Adelia was correct, their acquaintance had been brief.

While she might not remember him, he certainly remembered her. Eyes like hers came along once in a lifetime. They were unforgettable.

Of course, the last time he had gazed into them they were the eyes of a child.

In the moment he was gazing into the eyes of a woman.

Probably the most appealing and lovely woman he had ever seen.

Past and present collided, threw him off balance, made him feel half-flustered...in a rather nice way, though.

He only wished he had brought a larger bunch of dog rose.

It was a wonder she was still breathing. Ginny's heart thudded so hard against her ribs it was a bit of a miracle that her bodice was not jiggling.

Sitting in the back seat of the open carriage, she stared at the back of William's head where he sat beside the driver.

The other ladies being transported to Hawkwood chattered on about the beauty of the lake, the incredible blue of the sky and the rugged majesty of the fells.

Ginny was only grateful that her mouth was not hanging open.

But truly, she had expected to see William Talton and ought to have been prepared for the moment.

Oh, but how could she have been? In her mind, in her journal, he had never really aged, he only grew larger. The man sitting on the bench only feet away had grown. Oh, my, he certainly had.

The narrow shoulders of an adolescent had broadened. He had grown quite a bit taller and his slender frame transformed from lanky to muscular.

Although she could not see his face, she knew he had dimples, two of them. They had flashed playfully when he smiled at her a moment ago. Dimples were one thing about him that had not changed.

Curiously, her reaction to them had changed a great deal.

Back then those dimples made her heart flutter…now it was more than just her heart aflutter. Her tummy and her nerves were acting quite strangely.

What she wondered most about William Talton was, did he recognise her? Did he remember her at all?

Possibly he did not. She had changed as much as he had. Just because she recalled every detail of their day together did not mean he did.

It was foolish to hope so.

If William viewed her as anything other than

another woman coming to Hawkwood in hopes of winning his brother, she would be stunned.

And delighted. Still, that was one hope she did not dare entertain.

Besides, even if he did recognise her, it did not matter. It was Lord Hawkwood seeking a bride, not his younger brother.

Aunt Adelia had not brought her all this way, invested hours upon hours of teaching her to be socially at ease to have her give her attentions to anyone but the Earl.

Renewing old friendships was not her purpose here. Finding the courage to attract a husband was.

To that end, she pulled her gaze away from the play of sunlight dancing in William Talton's hair, from the shift of his wide shoulders when the carriage rolled over ruts in the road. She yanked her mind away from dreamily wondering what his laugh would sound like.

When she was twelve years old it had been the most engaging sound she had ever heard. It had warmed her and eased her grief.

'I have been told there is a splendid waterfall near the estate,' the Countess said.

'Aira Force.' Aunt Adelia nodded and smiled.

'It is a beautiful thing to see. You must make sure to visit it during your time in Ullswater.'

'I shall make sure to see it with our host,' Lady Della said with a giggle. In Ginny's opinion, the laugh was a bit suggestive.

Ginny thought William tipped an ear in their direction, but could not be sure since he also appeared to be listening to something the driver was saying.

'We shall all make the trip together!' Aunt Adelia waved one hand in the space between the facing seats. 'It will be grand fun. We will make a picnic of it.'

A picnic…and perhaps William would steal her away again and there would be a storm and—

Or perhaps she would be better off directing her thoughts to the here and now. To the man who was looking for a bride.

'Wouldn't that be a fine time, Virginia?' Clearly her aunt was trying to draw her into the conversation.

So far she had given the ladies seated across from her only the briefest greeting, her attention having been caught up in watching Lord Bold and Handsome in the flesh.

The grown-up, quite attractive masculine flesh.

What no one knew about Ginny was that while her demeanour was shy, her thoughts were not.

'Yes…that would be entertaining.' It was easier to smile at the women than it had been to smile at the gentleman her aunt had set in her path on the journey here. Which was odd since she could easily read resentment in Lady Della's green eyes.

For all that Lady Della was probably newly debuted, she lacked an aura of dewy innocence.

Her gaze at Ginny was quite wary.

Perhaps Ginny would have been more acceptable to the girl had she been wearing her spectacles.

Lady Della really had no reason to dislike her. As usual, she was being judged for her appearance.

Had she a crooked nose or a black patch over her eye Lady Della would still have judged her, only for a different reason.

In Ginny's opinion society was too focused on outward appearance. It was a person's character which mattered. Truly, what was the point of having a pretty face only to have it disguise an unkind heart?

Wasn't she a silly thing, preaching to herself when she ought to be making friends?

'I look forward to seeing Aira Force with both of you…and enjoying many good times together during our stay.'

'I fear a week in this beautiful part of the country will not be long enough.' Lady Robinn delivered a dramatic sigh. 'But perhaps the invitation to me and my daughter will be extended.'

'Oh, yes, wouldn't it be grand? Virginia and I will be here for at least three weeks. Our hostess is my dear friend, don't you know, and we have not seen one another in some time. We have more to get caught up on than one short week will allow.'

That bit of news did not appear to sit well with the Countess. Less well with her daughter.

If they held resentment towards her a moment ago, they now looked at her with glances of half-lidded hostility.

Well, it was not as if she had not seen looks of the sort before.

Since there was no potted plant to hide behind and her glasses were packed away, she drew upon the confident smile she had been practising, although she suspected it would work better on a gentleman than this debutante and her mother.

'I'm certain we will have a delightful time,' she said.

Indeed, had she spoken those words to a man, he would have looked beyond pleased.

The ladies across from her gave no response, not so much as a twitch of a lip.

At least Aunt Adelia gazed at her with pride. The tilt of her chin and the arch of her brow let Ginny know she had her aunt's approval.

Chapter Four

'What do you think, William?' Eyes sharp, lips pressed in a thoughtful line, his mother stood beside him, looking over the ladies assembled in the parlour after dinner. 'Will your brother approve of them? He promised to get away from the gentlemen and join us.'

'They are all lovely, Mother. He can hardly be disappointed.'

'Indeed, do you see Adelia's niece? Lady Virginia is uncommonly pretty.' Mother must have noticed his grin because her gaze fastened on him, sharp as a bird's…as a hawk's. He had always thought the expression fitted his mother given she was the Dowager Countess of Hawkwood. 'You keep those dimples to yourself, young man. She has come to win your brother's heart. Yes, as have all the ladies.'

William clasped his hand to his heart, giving

his mother a playfully heart-stricken grin. 'You did not invite them to Hawkwood for my entertainment, then?'

'Quite the contrary. You are to be their entertainment.'

'If you insist upon it, I suppose I can soldier through.' He shot his mother a wink, then bent to kiss her cheek.

'You are your father all over again, my dear young charmer.' A smile twitched one corner of her mouth, but her gaze did not soften. 'Every young lady is here for Phillip.'

'I wonder if the young gentlemen you invited are aware of it.'

'Never mind them.'

'Did you know I proposed marriage to Lady Virginia?'

It was worth mentioning if only to see the stunned expression on his mother's face. Violet Talton was not an easy woman to fluster so he thoroughly enjoyed it when he was able to.

'That is nothing to jest about.'

'No, I really did. Ten years ago when she was twelve years old. I can't imagine she remembers it.'

'I'm surprised you do.'

'I was sixteen and so it left an impression on my tender, romantic heart.' He had meant it, the proposal, with all the passion of a sixteen-year-old having his first flush of infatuation.

'Get along with you.' She arched her brow in the way that gave her an imperious look. Some people were cowed by the gesture, but William found it difficult to be intimidated by the woman who had cooed away his hurts and comforted his nightmares as a child. 'Go charm our guests on behalf of your brother.'

In the event, there was only one guest he had an interest in charming.

She sat beside Aunt Adelia, a glass of sherry cradled in her fingers, the crystal rim pressed to her lips.

All those years ago he'd been enchanted by her pretty smile, for all that it was as vulnerable looking as a fawn.

There was still that quality about it, but there was one very distinct change. Back then, her lips did not look like rose petals…dewy with a lingering touch of sherry.

She caught him looking at her and glanced quickly away.

He wondered why. Did she remember him and the day they had spent together?

It was not likely. A woman like her? She would have been wooed and courted dozens of times since he had made his youthful, innocent, and quite heartfelt, proposal.

For all that he enjoyed spending time with women, he had never offered marriage to anyone since. Never come close to doing so.

Better, he supposed to leave marriage to his brother. Phillip was a man meant to have a wife. William was a man to cheer him on about it... from a safe distance.

All at once the whisper of conversation faded.

Hawkwood had entered the room.

For all that William was assigned to entertain the ladies, once Phillip strode into the parlour he might as well have been a splat of colour on the wallpaper.

At his brother's grand appearance, feminine gazes latched upon his every move...heads leaned towards him to catch his every word and bask in his smile.

It was ironic, really, when he gave it a bit of thought. The brother who might prefer to do without the attention given to him, or rather to his title, was lavished with it while the brother who enjoyed socialising was left with no one to speak to.

Not that he minded terribly because…but wait!

Watching Phillip's smile shift from lady to lady, William did have to admit that his brother was giving a decent impression of enjoying it.

What a stroke of luck that the lady William wished to spend a few moments with was not among the admiring little group.

Ginny sipped her drink and gave his brother's grand entrance only a quick sidelong glance.

As luck would have it, the chair across from Ginny and Aunt Adelia was suddenly unoccupied.

Lowering into it, William pretended it was Aunt Adelia he wished to spend time with. It came back to him how shy Ginny was and he had no wish to distress her by making her his focus.

'I trust everything is to your liking here at Hawkwood, Aunt Adelia.'

'It is as lovely as ever. I am installed in my favourite chamber, the one with a view of the lake. And how thoughtful of your mother to give

Virginia the chamber beside mine. I could not be more pleased.'

'I hope you are comfortable, Lady Virginia. Is there anything you need to make your stay more enjoyable?'

Those wide, dove-like eyes settled upon him. 'Everything is lovely, my lord.'

If she remembered him or their day together, he could not read it in her expression.

It gave him a bit of a turn to think she did not. He was disappointed, but it was understandable, of course. And yet that day had been among the best of his life. The way they laughed so freely together was healing at a time when he believed no healing was to be found.

For that one day he had been carefree, joyful and hopeful the way he was before his father died. For those few hours he forgot to miss Father with every breath.

The same had been true for Ginny...at least he'd thought so at the time. Of course, if she could look at him without remembering, perhaps they had not shared what he thought they had.

At least Mother need not fear his young, impulsive proposal of marriage being accepted after all this time.

It made him smile, thinking of it now, how he had kissed her forehead...vowed to find her and marry her.

Young love...sweet love...what a tender moment it had been. He only wished he was not the only one to have a recollection of it.

Perhaps if he could get some time alone with her, he would ask outright if she remembered that day.

Tomorrow he was taking the ladies for a ride about the lake on the *Raven*. Perhaps he would find a way to get Ginny alone for a moment.

'Perhaps there will be a lady here for you, William.' Aunt Adelia smiled at him in the way she had of appearing imp and fairy godmother all in one. 'The Good Lord knows, if I were decades younger, those dimples of yours would... well, decades be dashed, they are quite attractive, young man.'

While it was gratifying to know a lady of such experience thought so, what did Ginny think?

Did he even want her to think what he hoped she did?

He shouldn't. Lady Virginia was here to possibly wed his brother.

But rekindling a friendship with this lovely woman would not be out of line.

Ginny set her glass down on the table with a pronounced clink, shooting a sidelong glance at her aunt. Apparently, what she thought was that her aunt had said something out of line.

'Mother has made it clear that, while I might entertain you ladies…' he included them both in his smile '…it is my brother's hand up for offer.'

'I adore Phillip, you know I always have, but I am not sure I am ready to be married again just yet. I shall leave it to the youngsters to win your brother's heart.'

'And do you wish to win his heart, Lady Virginia?'

She gave him a long thoughtful look.

'I do not wish to win your brother, as if he were a prize to be captured. What I do wish is to discover if we might suit one another.'

'Well spoken, Lady Virginia.' If it was up to him to pick a bride for his brother, in this moment she would be the one. There was nothing she might have said which would be more suitable. 'I wonder which of the others share your sentiment?'

'We can only hope they all do, Mr Talton.'

And there it was, proof that she had forgotten him. His Ginny would never call him Mr Talton…to her he had simply been William…Will, she had called him.

In the grand scheme of life, it didn't matter. Years had passed. They had grown up. But perhaps their friendship might be renewed. If Ginny were the lady his brother chose, they would even be family.

He would like that. His brother's happiness meant everything to him. A marriage between Phillip and Ginny would be just the thing… would it not?

He would be happy to welcome her as a sister… certainly.

But he was getting ahead of things. It was as she said. It must be determined whether they suited one another.

'It has been a pleasure speaking with you both,' he said. 'And now I must be about my mother's business… I see a young lady looking in need of company.'

'Be kind to the poor dear,' Aunt Adelia said with a shrug. 'You know it is my niece who will win the day.'

'We do not know that, Auntie. I have yet to

even speak to Lord Hawkwood. He might find the other ladies far more appealing.'

He might, if he were blind and a fool. Since his brother was neither of those, he would be captivated by Lady Virginia.

Over the years he had imagined her still a child...his Ginny. It was now time to put that away because she was clearly no longer that. From this point on she must be Lady Virginia Penneyjons, a woman who was meant, quite possibly, for his brother.

She might be the very one to finish the healing that had begun in Phillip's soul.

And yet, try as he might to be happy about it, he could not completely manage.

Because despite his intention to direct his thoughts otherwise, somewhere within the fetching lady was his Ginny.

'What a dear young man William is,' Aunt Adelia declared, setting her empty teacup aside and smiling while she watched him walk towards the unattended guest. 'It is a shame you do not remember him from the day we had our picnic in Nottingham.'

'Oh, but I do remember him.'

Not only did she remember him, but she was still drawn to him. What was there about William Talton that made her feel comfortable...relaxed...at ease?

Yes, all of those things...but at the same time on edge.

Which could only lead her to believe what she truly felt was confused.

'But, my dear, why did you not say so?'

'It was so long ago. I fear he will not remember me.'

Aunt Adelia tapped her chin in thought. 'It seems a shame to pass up a chance to rekindle a friendship, yet I wonder if it is for the best. It is Phillip we are here for, after all.'

'I'm not convinced I will even get the chance to have a word with the Earl. The others are all over him like...oh, never mind.'

'Flies.' Aunt Adelia narrowed her gaze upon the women who hovered about Lord Hawkwood with such intensity one could nearly hear a buzz.

'Bees to honey,' Ginny said.

'That is a kinder way to put it, but, yes... exactly that. I think he will be very relieved when you rescue him from it.'

'I do not know how I will get close enough

to accomplish such a thing…assuming he even wants to be rescued.'

'Why, Ginny Penneyjons, you do know how.'

Have William introduce her was what her aunt surely meant.

'He is involved at the moment.'

Glancing his way, she saw him laughing with the lady he had gone to entertain. It should not bother Ginny that she looked so merry. Merriment was the purpose of the gathering.

Had he not revealed that his mother had assigned him the task of keeping the ladies content while they awaited their time with Phillip?

Oh, but he did seem to be enjoying his task.

'Put what I have been teaching you to use. Go across the room and convince William Talton to give you an introduction. Being introduced by the Earl's brother will put you far in front the rest of the hopefuls, I imagine.'

'This is not a game,' she reminded her aunt.

'Of course it is…one that Lady Talton and I intend for you to win.'

'I beg your pardon? Lady Talton?'

'Never mind. I misspoke.'

Ha! When had Adelia Monroe ever misspoken? Surely this party had not been planned simply to match her and Lord Hawkwood.

That notion was a bit farfetched to be believed, so perhaps she had indeed misspoken. Truly, it made no sense. If Lady Talton intended Ginny for her son, why invite all the others?

'Go and charm your man. You know what to do.'

'William Talton is not my man.'

'I was speaking of Phillip.'

'Yes, well…of course you were. But I must first charm his brother in order to get to him, mustn't I?'

'Indeed.' Aunt Adelia made a shooing motion with her fingers. 'Now off you go.'

She stood up, fluffed her skirt then took a step…and a deep, fortifying breath.

Surely this was something she was capable of doing. She had practised speaking to strangers. Spent time in front of her mirror being charming and vivacious to her reflection.

How difficult could it be to make a request of someone who was not precisely a stranger?

Smile…it was the first thing to do. As a social tool it was unparalleled. She found that if she approached someone with a congenial expression, the conversation tended to fall into place more easily.

William had his back to her, but turned to look when the lady he spoke with shifted her gaze from his face to over his shoulder.

He was already smiling because he had been chatting happily with the young woman. But when he recognised Ginny something flashed in his eyes...gladness... She was halfway certain she had not imagined it, had not read into it what she wanted to see.

Oh, but Aunt Adelia was correct about his dimples, they were quite attractive...heart flutteringly so. Not that it was a surprise to Ginny.

They had quite captured her twelve-year-old self. The echo of that sweet crush tickled her heartstrings.

'Lady Virginia! How nice of you to join us,' he said.

To her credit, the woman standing beside William did appear to try to hide her disappointment at the interruption, although she only half carried it off.

'Have you had the pleasure of meeting Lady Elizabeth Gilmore?'

'I have not.' Ordinarily she would let the comment stand as it was…but she was trying to shed the shyness that made her conversations brief and to the point. She meant to burst from her cocoon like a butterfly…to flap about in colourful abandon…or something of the sort. 'But I have been hoping to. Our fellow guests are so preoccupied with meeting Lord Hawkwood I feared I would not have the opportunity to meet anyone. But when I saw you speaking with Mr. Talton, I thought it might be my chance so over I came.'

Those were a lot of words let loose at once. She hoped her nervousness did not show.

'I think I speak for Lady Elizabeth and myself when I say how glad we are that you did.'

Was he really? Or was he merely playing the part his mother assigned him to play?

She should not care. It was Phillip looking for a bride, not William. Apparently, that was something she was going to have to continue to remind herself. He was on her mind far more than he ought to be.

Truthfully, she did not even know who this man was, only who he had been ten years ago.

'Yes, you do speak for us both. It is lovely to meet you, Lady Virginia. I hope you will call me

Elizabeth. So far, besides William, you are the only person I have had the chance to meet. The others are caught up in...' Her gaze shifted to the ladies gathered about their host. She shrugged.

For some reason, a reason which made no sense at all, it bothered Ginny that Elizabeth called him William. It seemed awfully familiar when they had only just met.

If the two of them did find an instant connection, well...it was not Ginny's business. She wished them well.

'And please...you need not call me Lady Virginia... Virginia will do.' It was only her family who called her Ginny so she did not offer that informality.

In Ginny's opinion, Elizabeth might be someone Lord Hawkwood would find attractive. Truly, the lady was quite pretty with richly hued brown hair and eyes the shade of warm honey.

'William,' Ginny said, hoping she appeared charming and not absurd. 'Might I ask a favour?'

'You may ask anything.' The eyes of a charmer sparkled at her.

How, she wondered, were any of the women able to see Phillip when his younger brother was in the room?

'I wonder if…' Oh, this was a bold thing to ask. She glanced over at the couch, hoping for a nod of encouragement, but Aunt Adelia was speaking with Lady Hawkwood.

All right then, she would forge ahead without it.

'I wonder if you might provide me and Elizabeth an introduction to your brother.'

There, it was said…done. She would feel a good bit better about it if it were not for the nearly imperceptible sagging of his smile.

What a great humiliation it would be if he refused. She might never find the courage to boldly speak her mind again.

It seemed to take for ever for him to answer and all the while her heart beat madly and her stomach churned, but truly it was but a few seconds.

'Indeed.' When he nodded a lock of fair, golden hair slipped across his brow. He flicked it back with manly fingers which were a far cry from the boy William's long, gangly ones.

His hand so caught her attention that she nearly forgot she was waiting for a response to an important question, for both her and Elizabeth.

'I will be pleased to introduce you. Let me see

if I can disentangle him from his admirers. Wait here and I will bring him over.'

He went on his way, casting a smile back over his shoulder.

'It was kind of you to include me, Virginia. I could not think of how I was going to gather the nerve to approach him on my own.'

'Truly?'

'Yes, truly. I haven't an ounce of your confidence.'

That was a rather incredible thing to hear. Her confidence...of which she had none?

'If you knew me longer than a minute, you would see I have the nerves of a flea,' Ginny answered.

They looked at each other, blinking. Elizabeth's lips twitched...so did Ginny's. Within a second they were laughing quietly together over their shared lack of social courage.

'Would you believe that my Aunt Adelia—that is her over there, speaking with Lady Hawkwood—had me practise flirtation with a strange gentleman on the train ride from London?'

'My mother hired a tutor. She is determined that I shall wed the Earl and does not trust my natural charm to get the job done.'

'Oh, I think he will like you quite well.'

She was not certain why she should think so, given that she had only just met Elizabeth.

It was a hunch—that and feeling they would look splendid standing side by side.

Moving closer to her new friend, she watched William cross the room, then speak to his brother.

Phillip was a handsome man, the fact was plain to see. His dashing dark looks gave him a rather earnest demeanour. One only had to see his constrained smile to know he was not completely at ease with the attention of the ladies gathered about him.

Ginny barely remembered him from the long-ago picnic. And why would she? He'd been a man, only just learning to deal with all that came with his new title and she had been a child… a young, flutter-hearted girl enamoured of his younger brother.

Seeing the brothers together, blond head bent to rich deep brown, she felt somewhat disturbed because—

'The other gentlemen are returning.' Elizabeth muttered with a sad little sigh. 'We might miss our chance for a private introduction.'

A rumble of masculine voices ushered from

the hallway while William and Phillip continued on their way towards the hearth where she and Elizabeth waited.

'There is a woman with them! Do you hear her?'

It would be hard to miss the feminine voice rising in laughter over the lower tones of the gentlemen.

'I thought we had all arrived,' Elizabeth grumbled. 'It is rather rude of her to arrive so late.'

Thoughtless, at the very least. Just when their hostess had time to relax and enjoy the company of her guests, she might have to see one more settled.

The lady burst into the room with all the drama of a queen leading a gaggle of adoring knights.

Single gentlemen hovered about her navy-hued, satin-clad self. Married gentlemen's gazes shifted her way and lingered.

'I expect her bosom will pop out before the evening is over,' Elizabeth muttered.

Maybe, but it rather looked to Ginny as if it was already popped out. The gown was pretty, but it had a neckline lower than fashion called for and only a sheer film over the bodice to give the illusion of modesty.

The lady certainly did look dramatic with her gown undulating in a shimmer about her petite, trim figure. A strand of glossy, midnight-black hair curled down her neck, then across her bosom as if by accident. She twirled it in one fair-as-ivory finger, drawing attention to its placement.

The small black puppy she carried under one arm went nearly unnoticed.

Whoever this woman was she did not lack for confidence. Her smile, as she strode into the parlour, seemed to declare that now she had arrived, the rest of them might as well pack their bags and go home.

William turned to look at the newcomer. He nodded and smiled, but snatched his brother's elbow and continued towards Ginny and Elizabeth.

The Dowager stood. Aunt Adelia came to her feet a second after her.

'Lady Kirkwynd,' Violet Talton announced. 'How lovely of you to join us…at last.'

'I do apologise for my tardiness, Lady Hawkwood. I did hate to miss dinner, but I needed to see my maid settled and my team attended to in the stables. The horses are the highest notch and I had to be certain your grooms and mine agreed on their care. And sweet little Bernard needed to be walked. Your gardens are exceedingly lovely, by the way.'

Elizabeth tipped her head towards Ginny. 'I cannot believe she brought her own maid and livestock. And a dog? Really, has she never attended a country party? No one brings a dog.'

Well, Ginny could hardly say if she had or not, but it was customary to leave your animals and your staff at home so as not to burden your hostess. Bringing one's own ladies' maid might be acceptable, but—

'Besides, taking care of those matters would not take so long. She simply wanted to spend time with the gentlemen,' Elizabeth grumbled.

Perhaps it was true, but again, Ginny could not say. What Ginny could say was that Lady Kirkwynd knew how to make a grand entrance. Nearly every eye was focused upon her, the gentlemen's in appreciation, but the ladies were clearly piqued.

Especially their hostess, her lips pressed together in what could only be annoyance.

And then there was Aunt Adelia, smiling as

pleasantly as ever. What was really going on in her mind, Ginny could not begin to guess.

It should not make her feel so pleased that the Talton brothers were not giving their attention to the newcomer, but it did.

How could she not be anything but gratified when the Taltons stopped in front of her and Elizabeth? With a nod and a smile William appeared ready to give them the introduction to his brother.

'Lord Hawkwood!' Lady Kirkwynd hurried forward, insinuating her dark satin-clad figure between the brothers, her small pet's tail wagging madly. 'I know it is not quite the thing… I should wait for a proper introduction, but I declare I have not slept a wink since I received your invitation, my lord.'

The Dowager Countess and Aunt Adelia took places beside her and Elizabeth.

'It was my invitation, of course.' Lady Hawkwood levelled a cool glance at Lady Kirkwynd. 'Welcome to Hawkwood, Baroness. I am pleased that you were able to join us…at last. I had given up hope of having the pleasure. I can only assume your response to the invitation must have gone astray.'

'Did it? How unfortunate. I shall strive not to be a burden.'

'Indeed, I have faith my staff will rise to the occasion. May I introduce my dearest and oldest friend, the Marchioness of Montblue.'

Ginny glanced sidelong at William during the introduction. What did he think of the forward newcomer?

While it was none of her business to wonder what sort of woman Will had grown up to admire, she found it quite impossible not to wonder.

'What a delight it is to meet you, my dear.' Aunt Adelia gave the appearance of this being so. 'May I say how lovely you look this evening?'

With a nod the woman seemed to accept the compliment as her due, then she touched the strand of hair falling over her shoulder. She twirled it in her finger, tugging it towards her bosom.

'Oh, indeed, utterly lovely. It is a wonder your late husband is not rising from the grave in renewed lust,' muttered Lady Hawkwood.

The brothers stared at their mother with twin expressions of horror.

Aunt Adelia tapped her chin, a deceptively charming smile playing at her lips.

'I'm certain your pretty guest has caused a few of the gentlemen in attendance to rise, Violet. I can imagine our dear old friend Lord Helm has not felt such a lift of...of his spirits, in years.'

'Do you know,' the Baroness said smoothly, her gaze settled squarely upon the Earl, 'I believe I did hear a strange rustling noise when my carriage passed the churchyard near my home. I rather thought it was my dear, late Chester giving his blessing upon my emergence from mourning.'

'It appears that your emergence has been successful, Lady Kirkwynd.' Violet Talton took the Baroness's elbow. 'Come along, I'm certain your fellow guests are eager to make your charming acquaintance...and the dog's. He is not a snapper, I hope.'

Swept neatly away, Lady Kirkwynd cast one quick, coquettish smile back over her shoulder.

Ginny glanced again at William just in time to catch the return smile he shot the lady.

He could not possibly find her blatant flirting attractive! Young Will would never have fallen prey to such a tactic.

Although, Lord Bold and Handsome had succumbed upon occasion. Of course, he had been under the spell of a trollop so it hardly signified.

Hearing a deep, manly voice say her name, she looked up into the smiling face of Phillip Talton.

In spite of Lady Kirkwynd's theatrical entrance, Ginny had managed to get her and Elizabeth a private introduction.

Aunt Adelia gave her a wink, an acknowledgement that she had done well.

And she had! She had ventured on to a precipice, taken a leap and dared to speak up. And now look, she had what she wanted.

She had to admit to feeling rather grand.

It was amazing. A sense of victory over herself made her feel like dancing. So she did. Right there under her skirt she tapped her toes.

Chapter Five

The bedchamber of Adelia, Marchioness of Montblue

Adelia, my dear,
I am relaying my thoughts by pen and ink because I am too wound up to sleep. Truth be told, our plan...scheme, if you will...makes me feel as if we are girls again. I would not have expected that finding my boy a wife would be quite so much fun.

Lady Kirkwynd was perfection, was she not? While I do feel rather badly for inviting her, when we both know my son will dislike her blatant lavishness, she is useful beyond measure. Seeing the Baroness side by side with Ginny will make your niece shine all the brighter.

I suppose we must not feel too wicked

about our calculating invitation. And, really, what harm is done to her? She is having a grand time keeping the young swains trailing after her skirts. I have no doubt that at the end of this our families will be one. What could be better?

Even though you have yet to read this missive, I know what you are thinking. There are other young ladies present to whom Phillip might be drawn.

Rest assured. I have put great thought into the invitations. The gentlemen I have invited are all extremely eligible. They and the ladies are sure to form attachments to one another. The success of this party will be spoken about for years. Not only for Phillip and Ginny but for other betrothals made.

Sleep well, my friend, for in the morning we have a great deal of matchmaking to instigate.

A few things went right for William this morning.

For one, only five of Phillip's ladies had chosen to go on the boat ride around the lake. Virginia was among them.

For two, Phillip decided at the last moment to come along which relieved William of the responsibility of keeping the ladies entertained. He imagined the lay-a-beds were going to be distraught when they discovered what they had missed.

And three, given all the tourists in town for the one-year anniversary of the launch of the *Raven*, the Hawkwood group had managed to procure the last of the tickets to board. Which, as it turned out, was not the third piece of good luck.

No sooner had they found a place at the rail than a woman dashed frantically along the pier, calling out to be allowed to come aboard.

Baroness Kirkwynd waved her arms over her head in a wild gesture which set her ample bosom a-jiggle. While this might attract Phillip's attention, it was not likely to be in the way she hoped. In his opinion, she was not a good match for his brother. He could not imagine what had got into his mother to include her among the guests.

It was not for him to try to figure it out. No, right now it was for him to be grateful for this last bit of luck which was that Ginny volunteered to wait for the next tour about the lake so that

Lady Kirkwynd could board. Being a proper host, William waited with her.

It was an interesting thing about living in the country...social mores were loosened. With Mother's decision that the house party was to be relaxed, it was not likely that anyone would call him to task for being alone with Virginia. Although they were not truly alone—there were several people coming and going.

Then there was good luck number four which was not luck so much as it was pleasing. Virginia was wearing a flower tucked into her hair. If it was not the same one he gave her yesterday at the station, it was still a dog rose.

Pink petals echoed the blush in her cheeks. She carried her hat in her hand, allowing summer sunlight to reflect in her hair. Golden strands shimmered with a blush of strawberry.

Yesterday he had gathered bunches of dog rose because it was a common flower around the manor house. But there was nothing common about the way it looked peeking out of Lady Virginia's locks. To his way of thinking it was a kiss from nature resting just above her ear.

Phillip was a lucky man to have Lady Virginia Penneyjons competing for his heart, although she had made it abundantly clear that conquest was not something she was interested in, rather it was getting to know his brother.

Which was what William had in mind…getting to know her…again. How much did she recall of their day together, if anything at all? So far, she had not said anything that would give him a clue.

The boat whistle blew loud and deep. Members of their party waved from the deck as the *Raven* drew away from the dock. The Baroness did not wave her hand, her attention being caught up in attempting to capture Phillip's. Even from here his brother looked as if he would rather be speaking to Lady Elizabeth.

With the vessel now a hundred yards out across the water, he and Virginia walked back down the dock, the tap of their steps on the wood and the lapping of water on the pillars the only sounds.

Once upon shore, the twitter of birds became louder, the quack of ducks more pronounced. If the silence between them was any more strained, he might even hear fish swishing in the water. There had not been silence between them the day of the picnic when they were children. There was but one way to know what she recalled or did not recall.

Beside the water there was a shady tree with grass growing under it. The spot was several yards from the path where visitors took walking tours of the lake. The area was tranquil. If one listened closely, one could hear bees buzzing happily in the heather.

Given how busy Hawkwood had been of late, a bit of tranquillity would be welcome. He had always found it an odd thing that, as much as he enjoyed company, he also craved solitude.

This moment presented a perfect blend of the two.

'Shall we wait here in the shade?' he asked.

'Oh, yes.' Her smile felt like an echo from the past. 'This is one of the prettiest spots I have ever seen. I could sit here for ever.'

He spread his coat on the grass for her to sit upon.

'I wouldn't mind for ever, but I'd get hungry. Shall I get us a pie from the lad selling them over near the dock?'

'That would be splendid, thank you.'

Her words sounded polite, formal…but there was something in her smile, a tip of her lips which gave him hope that she remembered. But perhaps he was reading into it what he wished to—that they had sat by a stream eating pie once before. Ginny had a dab of it on her nose, he remembered. They laughed until their sides ached.

She might not recall it, he thought while walking towards the lad selling pies. It would hardly be one of life's tragedies if she did not. But if she did…well, it would be gratifying to speak of that long-ago day when they had cast their sorrow aside for a time.

Back again with the tasty-looking pie, he sat down beside her, setting the pretty treat down between them.

'The grass here is so fresh you can nearly smell green,' she commented.

'There's a poetic thought. You must have a way with words, Virginia.'

'I do dabble at writing…in a journal only.'

'Truly? What do you write about? Events of the day…current gossip?'

Whatever it was made her face flush and her fair throat grow red and splotchy.

'Just that…gossip and events.'

He'd wager that was not true. Now he was

intensely curious to know what it was she did write.

'What does the younger brother of an earl do to keep himself busy?' she asked in an abrupt change of topic.

'I held a naval commission for a time, but I never got used to being seasick. I had to resign.'

'How disappointing for you. I'm sorry to hear it.'

'Don't be. I'm landlubber at heart. Now I do everything at Hawkwood that my brother has no time for. Phillip is in London more than he is here so I suppose you might say I am the legs of the estate while he is the head. Then there is my mother, she is the heart of it.'

'May I ask you something?'

'I'll answer if I can.'

'It has to do with Lord Hawkwood. I understand that he is recently out of mourning and I was wondering if...this is a bit personal, so do not feel you must give me an answer, but you are his brother and understand him more than anyone does.'

Her lovely eyes rested upon him while she waited for some acknowledgement that it was appropriate to proceed with the conversation.

He nodded.

'Is your brother truly ready to be married again?' She turned her gaze out to the water, silent for a moment. 'It is just that, given the reason I and the others are here, it would be important to know. Is there hope of having a true marriage or will memories of his first wife make a new marriage simply the fulfilment of an obligation?'

Phillip was not the person he wanted to discuss, but her concern was a valid one, also one he could put to rest.

'My brother loved his wife deeply. He was truly bereft when he lost her. But the thing about Phillip is that he has a heart meant for love. He misses what he used to have and hopes to find it again. He told me he is ready and I believe him.'

The question in his mind was, was Virginia Penneyjons ready for marriage? He knew her to be a fine lady, but was she ready to commit her life to his brother and to Hawkwood?

'Well, that does put one concern to rest.'

What other concerns did she have? Apparently more than one. But it was not Phillip he wanted to speak of just now, so he said, 'Tell me about yourself. What is your life like in London?'

'Oh, well, my sisters are married. Cornelia was

wed only weeks ago and Felicia last December. My cousin, Peter, has been so involved in seeing us settled that he has yet to find a lady of his own. He could not come with me and Aunt Adelia because of business he had in London. Seeing all the ladies here wishing to make a match, I wish he could be here. But, of course, this is your brother's party.'

'But what of your life? What do you do to pass your days?' He served them both a slice of pie, presented on a napkin the lad had supplied. 'I imagine you have suitors at every turn.'

'Oh, that...yes. I do spend a good amount of time trying to avoid them.' She took a bite of pie, shook her head, frowning. The expression did not diminish an ounce of her beauty.

'Do you not wish to marry, then? If so, I can only wonder why you are here?'

'I do wish to marry, especially now that my sisters no longer live at home and I know my cousin will not find someone of his own until he sees me settled.'

'But why Phillip? Surely you can have your pick of men.'

'My pick? Yes, that is what I have been told, of course. But it is not at all true. Truly, Wi— Mr Talton,' she said, slurring his name. Perhaps it was because she was uncomfortable with the conversation. 'I have yet to meet a man who can see past this.'

She circled her face with a quick twirl of her hand. For some reason she looked disgusted.

'Past the scar on your cheek, or past the wart on your nose?'

She laughed. His heart tumbled.

'But it is much the same thing. If one bears an extreme appearance, people have a hard time seeing past it to the person inside. It can be quite discouraging.'

'You have a dab of blackberry on your nose,' he pointed out, hoping the comment would spark a memory. Ten years ago she had jam on the tip of her nose, too.

She swiped it away and then turned her gaze to the lake, a tiny smile playing at her lips.

'My aunt thinks highly of your brother and so here I am to find out if we will suit. That is the simple reason I am here.'

'Ah,' he said, following her gaze towards the lake.

One thing had not changed in ten years. Ginny still found William Talton easy to speak with.

So easy that she had nearly called him Will. Luckily, she caught it back at the last instant.

Really, she ought to be more cautious.

'Do you like ducks?' he asked, looking away from the lake and directly at her.

Why did he ask her that? Could it be that he remembered she did? Did he recall how they had laughed so uproariously over the awkward, waddling creatures?

'But of course. Show me the person who does not and I will show you a humourless soul.'

He stood up and reached a hand down to her. 'Come. There's a family of them near the shore.'

What she did next was the most natural thing in the world to do…and yet the most surprising.

Reaching up, she took his offered hand. She was on her feet before she realised that neither of them wore gloves. It was summer, so why would they? But really…it was as if Lord Handsome and Bold reached out and touched her, skin to skin.

The contact was brief, but it shot straight to her heart. He would not know that for years, he had existed only on the pages of her journal and now…well, he was touching her!

It was as if ink had sprung to life and she felt quite undone by it.

But there were ducks! Two adults, the male swimming and the female rising from a nest half hidden in weeds.

Coming into the open, she ruffled her feathers, giving a great squawk.

Waddling across the grass, she was adorably awkward, but once in the water she became graceful. She squawked again and carried on with the noise until a fuzzy duckling emerged from the nest. The ball of fluff dashed towards the lake, but stumbled. Five more did the same. They tripped over each other until they resembled a chirping black and yellow heap, too confused to untangle from each other and follow their mother.

William squatted down, gently separated them and then carried them one by one to the water's edge where they slipped into the water and paddled after their parents.

All but one. William cupped the duckling in his palms and then carried it to her.

'Would you like to hold it?'

She made a cradle of her hands. The hatchling felt the softest thing she had ever touched. She nuzzled its tiny round head with her nose. It smelled sweet and babyish.

She glanced up, smiling at the man. To her great surprise it was the boy she saw grinning back at her.

Just like then, his dimples flashed. The timbre of his laugh was deeper now, but at the heart of it, it was no different.

'Thank you, Will. Isn't it the sweetest thing?'

'You do remember, then?'

'Of course I do.' She carried the duckling to the water, then knelt to set it on the grass. Hopping into the water, it scurried after its family, leaving small ripples in its wake.

She glanced over her shoulder and caught the grin on her friend's face. 'I have been waiting these ten years for you to find me and fulfil your promise of marriage.'

How surprising it was to discover she could slip so easily back to the time when they were naturally free and at ease with each other.

It was not quite the same, of course. Ten years ago there had been such innocence to their day alone...to the kiss on her forehead and even to the sweet proposal...yes, especially that.

'Had I known you were waiting, I'd have jumped ship and come straight away. Although I do wonder what your cousin would have had to say about it. A twenty-year-old sailor come to whisk away his sixteen-year-old charge.'

'It would have been quite the scandal.'

'But truly, Ginny, I am glad you remember me.'

Had he any idea how well she did he would be stunned.

'I'm glad you remember me, too.' She watched the duck family swim in a circle not far from shore.

'I would have said something right away, as soon as I recognised you, but I confess I did not want to know it if you had forgotten me,' he said.

'Truly? That is why I didn't speak up.'

The confession made them both laugh.

Sitting at the water's edge, he took off his shoes, then stripped off his socks.

Glancing up, he smiled that smile of his…only not the adolescent's smile. This was a man's smile and it made her stomach melt rather than flutter.

What lady would not react to such a dimpled, playful grin?

She would not allow herself to believe she still had a crush on him…how silly. What she felt was pleasure in knowing he remembered their time together. Friendship, pure and simple, was all she felt.

'You've seen my feet before and I've seen yours. Let's go wading.'

'No splashing, though.' Oh, but would it not be fun? 'The staff has enough to occupy their time without having to revive my gown.'

'Just a little splash?' Truly, the man could charm a snake out of a basket and it would deliver a kiss rather than a bite.

'It would be thoughtless, so, no.' He was going to splash, regardless. His eyes told her as much. 'All right, we shall challenge each other for the biggest splash...out that way towards the lake.'

'I accept your terms.'

He kicked before he was finished speaking. A great spray of water winked in the sunlight.

She had to lift her skirts higher than was quite proper to keep them dry and at the same time deliver the greatest power to her splash. Naturally, her stockings were getting soaked, but she was no longer that barefooted girl and would leave them on no matter what.

Drat it! His kick had more power than hers did. She would have to try harder.

Kick after kick she tried to best him and although she got in more splashes, his were larger and more dramatic.

But it didn't matter. Years fell away. They laughed together just as they had then. Ginny and Will, laughing away grief, if only for an afternoon.

In the end he admitted defeat, even though he had earned victory.

'Ginny Penneyjons, you are still the most playful girl I know. I swear I have not had such fun since I last saw you.'

'Funny how we went right back to that time. Once a friend always a friend, they say.'

'They do? Who says it?' He looked doubtful.

'Someone must say it because it seems to be true.'

'Indeed.' Damp hair splayed across his forehead, clinging to one cheek, making him look more dashing and adventurous than he usually did. 'I'd like to ask something of you.'

'I'll answer if I can.' She repeated his words from earlier.

'I'd like to keep calling you Ginny.'

'I would like that too, so, yes, please do call me that.'

'And you will call me Will?'

'You have always been that to me, Will.'

'Does that mean you thought of me over the years?'

'A time or two.'

'Who knows, Ginny? We might be related soon. I, for one, would like that.'

'It is a bit soon to know whom your brother will fancy.' And truthfully, something about being Will's sister felt off...a bit wrong.

Oh, but today had been fun...and Will was once again her friend.

Ginny rolled her shoulders, took a long breath and let it out slowly. At last she was settled at the writing table in her chamber with her journal open before her, pen in hand.

It had been a full day, the best part being the time she spent at the lake with Will. The rest of it had been rather nice as well. Walking in the garden with the other ladies, having afternoon tea served outside. Then later, after dinner, watching other young ladies dally in flirtations with eligible gentlemen. It left her to wonder how sincere their attentions towards the Earl were.

A few times today she'd forced herself to boldly walk up to a group of women already conversing. Inserting herself among them still made her palms sweat, but at least she did not blush at her intrusion.

There was also Elizabeth—spending time with her was easy and enjoyable. She had even asked her new friend to call her Ginny.

With the social goings-on she had spent little time with her aunt. Not that she feared Adelia Monroe lacked for company. Auntie, Violet Talton and Lord Helm had been friends since their youth and were greatly enjoying being in one another's company.

But now, here she was at the end of the day, grateful to close it as she usually did by writing a short, romantic adventure.

She stared at the page, pen poised and ready.

Something was wrong. Normally words sprang to her mind quicker than she could scratch them across the paper.

That was odd. Perhaps she needed to get up for a moment, think of something else and then come back to it.

Going to the window, she drew back the curtain, gazing out at the huge stretch of lawn leading to the lake's edge.

What a grand and breathtaking sight. A full

July moon shone brightly down to paint a silver path on the water's surface. And the stars...well, what could one say to do justice to the sparkling canopy?

A gentleman stood beside the water...oh, wait, another figure, a young lady, hurried to join him.

The two of them stood nearly shoulder to shoulder. She could not tell who they were from here, but apparently a mild flirtation begun earlier in the evening was about to go a step further.

Not wishing to eavesdrop, she started to turn away from the window, but another couple emerged from the house.

Closer to her window, it was easy enough to identify who they were.

Lady Kirkwynd's sultry laugh carried up. The gentleman walking beside laughed in answer. She recognised him by his gait. The set of his shoulders and his manly stride...it was Will, of course.

Well, it certainly appeared to be an evening meant for romance. She watched for a moment longer than she ought to because...well, she just did.

If Will held a *tendre* of some sort for the Baroness, it was no business of hers.

But perhaps he did not and was simply following his mother's instructions to keep the ladies entertained.

She turned abruptly from the window because the last thing she wanted to know was how he meant to keep this one entertained.

It really was not her concern. Had it been Phillip down there with Lady Kirkwynd, perhaps that would be her business. She would need to be aware of it if he were developing a connection with another lady.

As of yet, she had not had a lengthy conversation with the Earl. The last thing she wanted was to interfere with someone who had…another lady who might be more suitable for him.

'Well,' she huffed, 'I have fictional characters to attend to.'

She sat down once more, picking up her pen. Drat it if her gaze did not wander to the open window.

For this late in the evening there was plenty of activity going on outside. But there was the full moon and—

Very well, she touched her pen to the paper.

'By the light of a full moon reflecting off the

water like a strand of pearls, Lord Handsome and Bold...what?'

Something was quite wrong. Her hero of many years was not right. His image had always been so clear in her mind. But now it was blurred.

A few days ago it had been as sharp as a flesh-and-blood person's would be.

This was most unsettling.

'Justina?'

Ah, at least she remained as she always had... admirable and ready for adventure.

And yet the more she tried to picture the young hero Justina was meant to adventure with, the fuzzier he became.

She suspected the gangly youth might have outgrown the pages of her journal.

Setting the pen aside, she rose and went back to the window. There was no one out there now, only the lake and the moon involved in an intimate rendezvous.

Looking out, she suspected that Lord Handsome and Bold was dead, never to be revived.

Now that Ginny was reunited with the man who had been his inspiration, everything was changed.

She could only liken it to when one imagined

a place one was to visit and had vague images of what it would look like. Then, once visited, the visions were replaced with what was real. The imagined faded quickly, never to be recalled.

'Goodbye, Lord Handsome and Bold,' she whispered.

And then she smiled because Will was so much more interesting as a real man than a fictional one.

Poor Justina Admirable was going to have to get along as best she could...or perhaps even retire.

After one last, lingering gaze out the window, she returned to the writing table and snapped the journal closed...for good.

Or perhaps only until she could think of something else to jot down in it. She did find fulfilment in writing, after all.

She would have expected to feel more remorseful about leaving her characters behind, but instead she felt a tingle of excitement for the future.

Whatever that future might be, it had to be more exciting than the black and white scribbling of the unlikely adventures of a childhood crush.

Readying for bed, she determined to look towards that future, not back at the childish affection she felt for a friend. And she did feel affection for that boy…for the memory of him.

But a memory did not make a future.

No, indeed. What she was looking for was a relationship with a man.

To that end, tomorrow she was going to find a way to spend time with Phillip Talton.

Chapter Six

The next day, after lunch, Ginny stood with the ladies, watching gentlemen shoot at targets.

It was a fine afternoon for it, if rather warm. Fortunately, a mass of white clouds pushed over the fells to relieve the heat.

Lord Hawkwood assured everyone that even though it was unusually warm for Ullswater, he thought a storm was brewing and would bring some relief.

Ginny truly hoped so. The high neck of her gown and yards of fabric were suffocating. All she could think of was how wonderful the cool lake water had felt during yesterday's splashing contest.

There had been no loser in the competition since fun had been the prize and they had both experienced a great deal of it.

'Come along, Ginny.' Aunt Adelia cut into her

thoughts. 'It is time you had more than a "how do you do" with our host.'

Looking past the targets, she spotted Lord Hawkwood standing under a tree near a rose-bush abloom with the same flowers William had given her…all right…her and every other lady he had picked up from the train station.

It seemed important to remember that he had presented them all with the same gift. The flower had been a cordial greeting and nothing more.

What had possessed her to place one of the blooms in her hair yesterday? Well, it was pretty and she would admit to no other reason.

Lord Hawkwood had his head bent towards his mother, listening to something she had to say. He nodded, looked up, then glanced around. His gaze settled on Ginny. He smiled.

If she did not know better, she would think she had been the subject of his conversation with his mother.

But of course, that could not be. It was only her self-conscious nature making her think so.

'Quickly, before one of the others spots him unattached.'

Snatched by the elbow, Ginny hurried along beside her aunt. She ought to be grateful for Aunt

Adelia's assistance. Speaking with the Earl was what she had wanted to do, only she hadn't the mettle to approach him on her own.

Apparently, Lady Kirkwynd suffered no such handicap. Spotting Phillip Talton with no companion except the Dowager, she abruptly turned away from the gentleman she had been entertaining, Lord Helm it was, who appeared a bit taken aback by her sudden departure.

'Perhaps later, then,' Ginny mumbled, halting several feet behind a fellow taking aim at the target.

The last thing she wanted was to have to compete for the Earl's attention. She doubted he would even see her, not with having the engaging widow to speak with.

Aunt Adelia did not seem to care what she wanted because she continued her forward progress, causing Ginny to lurch suddenly forward.

'Nonsense. Look, there is Violet going to chase the chit off.'

But why would she? The 'chit' had been invited to Hawkwood for the same reason the rest of them had.

The next man waiting his turn to shoot was William. With his rifle resting on his shoulder, he grinned and winked while she was towed past him.

In under a moment she was standing with the Earl under the shade of the tree. A scent of roses wafted from the bushes. The fragrance was extra sweet because of the warmth of the day.

It was a lucky thing Aunt Adelia began the conversation because Ginny had quite lost her tongue now that she was face to face with the Earl…a man who was weighing each girl…her in this very moment…and deciding who would best suit his needs as Countess.

It was not likely to be Ginny since a countess must be a woman of great social grace, comfortable in the company of strangers, easily engaging everyone she encountered.

No, indeed. This was not Ginny Penneyjons. Why on earth had her aunt ever entertained the idea that she would suit Hawkwood?

'Aren't they lovely?' she said of the roses because she needed to say something, for pity's sake.

'Quite.' His voice went soft. 'They were my late wife's favourite.'

'May I say, my lord, how truly sorry I am for your loss?' This came quite naturally because she was speaking from her heart and not looking for some witty and trite thing to say.

'Thank you, Lady Virginia.' He nodded once, then smiled. It was a genuinely nice smile, she thought. Warm and friendly. All at once she did not feel she was in the presence of a title, but of a human being. 'It was a bitter thing, losing Cora. But she would want me to go on. Would insist upon it, in fact.'

'I can only imagine what a lovely lady she must have been.' She was certain of it or Phillip Talton would not be where he was now, which was hopeful of finding new love.

'Oh,' she exclaimed. 'Apparently my aunt has deserted us without a word.'

'I cannot say I am surprised.'

The Earl was as handsome as his brother, only in a quite different way. Lord Hawkwood seemed sober minded and yet not starchy. His smile was engaging without being…well, quite frankly, without being dimpled. His darkish good looks seemed to fit his more sober position as Hawkwood.

How interesting it was, one brother with a warm, congenial smile and the other with a grin which encouraged a person to laugh out loud.

Shade and sunshine was how she saw them, each wonderful in their own way.

'Both my mother and Aunt Adelia are match-makers to the bone. I'm sure it has not escaped you that this gathering is meant for more than a delightful week in the country.'

'My aunt did mention such was the case.'

Lord Hawkwood laughed quietly, nodding while he did. 'I must say, it is rather flattering having so many fine ladies seeking my attention. I've not experienced anything like it before.'

'But you do not find it overwhelming?' Interestingly enough, she found speaking with Phillip quite easy, not a bit stilted. It must be a Talton trait, putting people at ease.

'It can be, of course. I am aware that most women are attracted to my title and not my charming self. Not that I am judging you or anyone else, it is simply the way of it when one is among society's peers. But perhaps I shall recognise a lady who suits in spite of it.'

'I do know something about...well, never mind.' She'd only just met the man and was not ready to confide her whole heart, for all that he was quite approachable. 'But I have every confidence you will find a lady among the party who will suit. And if you do not, there is no great rush to wed, I would imagine.'

'Mother would say otherwise. In fact, she has on several occasions.'

Her gaze wandered to where Will stood, aiming his rifle at a target. With his natural, masculine grace, he was probably an excellent shot… not that masculine grace had so much to do with it as an accurate eye, but—

'Shall I let you in on a secret, Lady Virginia?'

She jerked her attention back to where it ought not to have wandered from.

'You may count on my discretion.' Hopefully this was not a huge and tempting secret.

'My brother has promised to help me sort out who will suit and who will not. He has always been sociable, at ease in the company of ladies. It is a quality which I do not possess.'

'Nor do I, my lord. The words sociable and at ease cannot be used in relation to me. Although my aunt is doing her utmost to cure me of it.'

'Truly?' His brows rose in question. The expression made him look more boyish. Perhaps out from under the weight of the responsibilities he carried he was more like William than he seemed. 'I would not have guessed it about you.'

'Only because I find it easy to speak with you, the same as I do your brother.'

'William? But...yes, I recall it now. It was you he was lost in the storm with all those years ago.'

'I'm surprised you remember it.'

'It is only because I had just become Earl and felt rather dramatically that I was now responsible for everyone. I told Mother I would look for you, but she said it was too dangerous and as long as you were with William you would be perfectly safe. For all he has an easy way about him, my brother has always been dependable. It is why I never worry when I must spend long periods of time in London.'

Her mind flashed back to that storm...to sheltering in the cave and William asking if she was scared. 'I'm here so you needn't be.' She heard the echo of his adolescent voice rather clearly in her heart.

'I do not like storms and that one was dangerous, but the odd thing was I never did feel afraid. William helped to make a pleasant day of it.'

A pleasant day which she had not forgotten although more than ten years had passed...more than three thousand, six hundred, and sixty-five days. Why on earth would she know that? She had a brilliant memory…but really, she did not recall everything as clearly as that day.

Because she held that day in her heart, cherished it and smiled over it, was why.

She sighed inside where only she knew it. For all that she wished to never forget a second of that time in the cave, she was here at Hawkwood to create new memories.

Regardless if Phillip Talton chose her or not, she would make them good memories since apparently, they would be with her for a quite a long time.

From the corner of her eye she saw two women approaching.

'I have so enjoyed speaking with you, my lord, but here comes Lady Elizabeth and Lady Kirkwynd and I have taken more than my share of your time.'

'It has been my pleasure speaking with you, Virginia, truly, I do mean that. And I hope I may address you informally?' He glanced at the ladies rushing towards him, pressing his lips together. 'I wonder what my brother will report about them?'

She could not help but laugh because she really would not wish to be in the Earl's position.

Or perhaps not Lady Kirkwynd's, either. Try as she might to get to their host before Elizabeth did, her small dog was latched on to her skirt, playfully growling and yanking.

'I think he will have nothing bad to say about Lady Elizabeth. The question in my mind,' she added because she had to wonder, 'is what he will report about me.'

Now it was the Earl's turn to laugh. 'Perhaps I should not have let the secret slip.'

'Well, now that you have, I shall strive to be on my best behaviour.'

She backed away, covering a smile because it was a humorous sight, the Baroness hurrying along, but at the same time attempting to free her skirt of the puppy teeth latched on to the ruffle.

Rain pelted the library window while William leaned against the frame, sipping port and listening to thunder roll across a dark, grumbling sky.

With the guests retired, he was now free to have a private word with Phillip, revealing his thoughts on the ladies.

'You've met them all by now,' William said. 'First you tell me what you think. After that I will let you know what I have learned so far.'

Phillip, half reclined on the couch, ankles crossed and three buttons of his shirt comfortably freed, lifted his glass.

They drank, enjoying the quiet moment before getting down to the business of finding Phillip a wife.

'First off, I don't know how many of them will be unattached by the time I come to a decision. It appears that the young men are pairing up with my prospects rather quickly.'

'That is true of a few of them. But when it comes down to it, they might choose a title over romance. If you want my opinion, a lady making such a decision would not be for you. But you do have several other ladies to choose from.'

Phillip sat up straighter. 'Lady Della is engaging and also quite pretty.'

'The problem with Lady Della is that she is competitive with the others. It is to be expected to some degree, of course, but I wonder if you ought to consider some other ladies before her.'

'Even Lady Kirkwynd? She is brazen...flashy. Still, she is quite beautiful. Yet I cannot say I am comfortable with how she flaunts her looks.'

'My sense is that there is more to her than what one sees. Almost as if she is hiding some sort of vulnerability behind all that brass. I did have a pleasant time walking by the lake with her last night. I honestly found her to be enjoyable company.'

'Enjoyable, was she?' Phillip chuckled under his breath. 'Feel free to enjoy her all you like, Brother. I fear she is not meant for me.'

'I did enjoy her company, only not in the way you are suggesting. But I do agree, she is not for you.' William shifted his gaze towards Lake Ullswater, saw a jag of lightning nearly touch the water. 'The Baroness is not for me, either, and even if she was I would not pursue her. This is your debut back into society, these are your ladies to choose from. I would never press my affections.'

'What if you did fancy one of them, though?'

'It would not matter since I am not the one to be wed.'

'Do you never think of it? Surely you must.'

He did, sometimes…and then he remembered Cora, how devastated his brother had been over losing her. He also remembered how long it took for Mother to learn to go on without Father.

Those were wicked, dreadful times for William, too.

Had it not been for the afternoon he spent with Ginny Penneyjons, he did not know how he would have managed those awful days after his father died. Somehow, being with her, taking a step back from grief for a time and replacing it with laughter, had been healing.

At this time in his life, was he willing to invest his heart so fully in someone…in a wife? He was not certain. Perhaps it was better to enjoy a woman's company for a while and then say goodbye.

Although Phillip, who had been through the worst with Father and Cora, was ready to take the risk again, so perhaps William was wrong.

Perhaps his problem was that he had yet to meet the lady to make the risk worthwhile.

Until he did…if he did…he would keep his heart to himself. Seeing Phillip move on with his life and find happiness once more would be enough for him.

'Hilde is pleasant, so is Maureen,' William continued, going over the women in his mind, one by one. 'Elizabeth is one who stands out to me. Of them all she seems the most genuinely smitten…with you more than Hawkwood. For as sudden as it is, I feel her interest in you is sincere. I have yet to see her entertain the flirtations of other gentlemen.'

'Yes, she is quite sweet. But tell me, what do you know of Virginia? This is not your first meeting with her.'

Oddly, he felt reluctant to present Ginny for his brother's approval.

'We were but children then, so it hardly counts.' It hardly counted for what Phillip needed to know. But that day he spent with Ginny counted to William…more than a little bit. If it hadn't he would not have carried the memory close to his heart over the years. But it was as he said, they had been but children. 'I like her, Phillip. She is shy, but under it she is someone whom you might consider.'

'Shy? She did not seem so when I spoke to her this afternoon. I found her to be quite engaging.'

Not shy? Of course she was shy! It was only in William's company that she was not.

He had the oddest sensation in his gut. He had never been jealous before, but this uneasy squeeze might be it.

There was no reason for him to be jealous. What he wanted was for his brother to find happiness with the right woman.

If it turned out to be Ginny, William would rejoice at Phillip's good fortune. Yes, that was exactly what he would do.

No matter if his choice was the Baroness, Ginny, or even Lady Della, he would be pleased for his brother.

'I like Virginia. I have never known her to be anything but unfeigned.' But there was this to be considered. 'And yet, she does not look at you the way Lady Elizabeth does.'

His heart went still for a moment, his breath caught in his lungs as he realised that he might like to be looked at that way. It gave his gut the oddest turn.

With a nod, Phillip finished his port in one long swallow.

'You have given me quite a lot to consider.' He stood up. 'I bid you good night, Brother... although with all you have told me I wonder if I will get any rest.'

William remained in the library, thinking about something he had just told his brother.

It had to do with the way Elizabeth looked at Phillip.

Not that the way any of Phillip's ladies looked at his brother should matter to William.

So why did it?

Ginny. Her name scratched at his heart. His gut turned again, but this time it twisted...ached.

He shook his head. He'd meant what he said when he told Phillip he would not pursue any of the ladies.

Not even the one who was trespassing into his thoughts...especially not her.

William was not the one looking for a bride and if he were—

But he was not and so he might as well go up to bed and put his confusion to rest.

Things would become clearer with the light of day.

Thunder was a beast pounding and stomping about the sky like a giant wearing lead boots.

Since Aunt Adelia's room was silent Ginny could only guess her aunt was sleeping contentedly through the bluster.

Perhaps there would be some relief down below. Putting two storeys between her and banging thunder could only help. Since she was still dressed, she decided to go to the library. Lady Hawkwood had offered the space to any guest who desired to make use of it, after all.

Since she was not likely to get a dash of sleep, she would spend her time within the pages of a book. Or perhaps she would encounter another guest undone by the elements.

Well then, wasn't that an encouraging thought... hoping to run into another person? A very short time ago she would have dreaded coming upon anyone she would be required to speak with.

Aunt Adelia's lessons were beginning to bear fruit.

Going downstairs, she turned right down one long hallway and then right again down a shorter one.

Since she had not encountered anyone, she would find a book to read and save the challenges of socialising for tomorrow.

Four doors down, she spotted the library.

Something odd happened when she reached for the doorknob. It turned before she touched it.

'Ginny!'

Will! How interesting that his smile could still make a storm seem less threatening.

'Hello, Will. I was just coming for a book since everyone is abed and I cannot sleep. This...' she waved her hand towards the window in the same second a flash of lightning turned the panes electrified white '...is unsettling. I thought I might distract myself with something to read.'

Thunder rolled over the lake, shivering the glass. The storm had to be directly over them.

'I'm not abed. You may distract yourself with me if you wish to.'

He would be more distracting than the best of fiction. Indeed, she had recently made that discovery. It led to the downfall of her journal.

In the moment, a diversion from foul weather was precisely what was called for.

Ten years ago, Will had turned such a maelstrom into fun. But then, ten years ago, she was only twelve years old and the pitter-patter of her heart had been sweetly innocent.

Sitting down on one end of the couch while Will sat on the opposite was...well, she did not know exactly what it was, but it was not what she'd felt sitting shoulder to shoulder with him at the mouth of the cave.

'You might guess, I still dislike storms,' she admitted.

His grin flashed. Gradually tension drained from her chest and limbs.

'I still like them.'

'I cannot imagine why anyone would.' She shot

him a look suggesting quite strongly that she considered his thinking to be illogical. 'A person could be struck by lightning...gone without even knowing what happened to them.'

'I can only think I would rather not know if it happened to me.' The teasing spark in his eye settled her, made her apprehension of the weather seem foolish. 'Believe me, Ginny, you are perfectly safe sitting here on the couch.'

Yes, perhaps...but safe from what, she wondered. This man was still Will, the friend from her childhood, and yet he was not. If then he had wanted to kiss her, she would have giggled and offered her hand, or perhaps even her cheek.

What would she do now...in the unlikely event the opportunity...well, not that so much as the unlikely happenstance, she meant...presented itself? Which it would not because...it just would not.

Now would be the time to send her thoughts elsewhere because, no longer being twelve years old, she might be tempted to offer something else to be kissed. The idea was far from appropriate given the reason she was visiting Hawkwood.

When, exactly had she become a wanton? Will was innocently speaking of the weather while her mind wandered vastly far afield. Or close afield, as it were, since he was sitting only feet away.

'Tell me about you and your brother growing up,' she said, grateful to find a safe topic to steer her thoughts towards. 'Did you have grand adventures together?'

'We might have had, but since he was four years older it was more as though he was constantly snatching me out of trouble.'

'Trouble… Tell me you were not a scamp!'

'You know I was. Did I not convince you to run away from the picnic and then I got us caught out in weather much like this?'

'You could not have convinced me to do anything unless I wished it. You may rest assured I was not led astray, but went with you quite happily.'

'Good, then.' His dimples relaxed with the softening of his smile. 'I used to wonder what you thought about it all, given time and distance. I feared you might blame me for putting you in danger.'

Danger! What she had been in danger of was diving headlong into grief over her parents' deaths. Will was the one who pulled her back from it…made her laugh instead of weep.

'What kind of trouble did Phillip pull you out of?'

'Ah, well…mischief mostly. Stealing eggs from the hen house and throwing them at the sheep…not to hurt them, you understand, but to see if they would open their mouths and catch them. They never did. The best I got was when one of them batted an egg with the nub of its tail. Then another time, I found an abandoned fawn so I brought it home to live under my bed. Phillip discovered it, though, and he made me take it back to where it belonged. I didn't know that mother deer left their newborns alone in order to direct predators away from them.'

'None of those things sounds so awful.'

'I've yet to tell you about what happened at Aira Force. It's a waterfall close by.'

'I've heard it is beautiful. We are picnicking there tomorrow, I believe?'

He nodded. A hank of blond hair fell across his brow and he swiped it away.

'As long as the weather clears, but I imagine it will. Summer storms do not last long. The worst of my mischief had to do with the falls.'

'Did you toss eggs over it?'

When he shook his head the hair slipped back.

This time he did not shove it into place, but left it to lie across his forehead, making him look every bit a mischievous boy.

'Myself...or nearly at least. One day I decided it would be a fine thing to ride over the falls in a whisky barrel. I would not be sitting here with you tonight had Phillip not wondered what I was up to and followed me. I was in the barrel at the head of the falls, thinking I could probably make it down alive. All it would take was a tip and over I would go for the ride of my life. Phillip caught me by the shirt collar and yanked me out. The barrel went over without me in it. Even now I get a chill remembering how it ended up a pile of splintered planks.'

'I had no idea you were such a rascal. May I trust you have outgrown that kind of mischief?'

A lopsided grin was his only answer. Apparently not, then.

'Tell me, Ginny. How did you get on when we parted ways?'

'I went on as one must. It hurt...you will know that, Will...but I learned to live without my parents, in as much as that is possible. Things did get better. I had my sisters and my cousin,

Peter. Together, we found our way back to happy times.'

'But your sisters have married.'

'Yes.' She sighed, thinking about how lonely Cliverton would be once Aunt Adelia returned home and it was only her and Peter in residence. 'But it is the way of things. I am happy for them both.'

'And so here you find yourself hoping to wed Phillip.'

'Hoping to discover if we might suit.'

He gazed at her without the customary flirtatious humour lighting his expression. 'But I wonder, Ginny…why have you not married already? Not for lack of offers, I imagine.'

Certainly not for that reason, alas. There had been offers, all of which she rejected because she was certain none of her suitors saw past her appearance. When a fellow proposed after a day, it could only be assumed it was her face he was enamoured of. Indeed, a face that would change over time, not always be young and fresh. What she wanted was a man who wanted her…the person on the inside.

'You needn't answer,' he said, no doubt taking

her silence as an indication she was unwilling to speak of something so personal.

And he was not wrong. For some reason, she felt reluctant to delve more deeply into her reasons for rejecting her suitors.

That was confounding. Maybe because when it came to Will, her feelings ran deeper and were more complicated.

'How could I marry? I was waiting for you to come and find me. It is what you promised, after all.' A dash of light-heartedness was called for since this conversation was more intense than she wished it to be.

Apparently he took her clue, for his answer was playful.

'You waited for me? Even after I failed to kiss you to seal the proposal?'

'So it would appear. But you did kiss me… right here.' She tapped her forehead, but that was not where he was looking.

The oddest warmth flushed her mouth since that was where he was staring rather intently. Surely he was not considering doing it now… not after all this time and distance?

Although the distance between them on the couch was not as great as it had been a second ago. How had that happened? Either he had leaned closer to her or she had tipped in his direction.

She felt the heat of his breath in the space between them.

Suddenly he blinked. So did she. They slid away from each other.

'Looks as though it was my brother I was proposing for without even knowing it.' His grin brought everything into sharp focus. 'As I see it, he owes me a favour.'

'What sort of favour?' she asked, relieved to have the conversation back on a proper topic.

'I would have him pay his due by giving me a faster horse than he has. We enjoy racing each other and now that he is himself again, he's getting better at it. I'm in danger of losing to him.'

'And you do not care for losing?'

'Not any more. I used to do it on purpose to make him feel better. I'd ask you not to reveal it, but I imagine he already knows.'

'I can see that you and your brother care deeply for each other.'

'Yes, but it might have gone the other way, I imagine, given that we are not at all alike.'

'Maybe it's better when we are not like our siblings. I'm nothing like Felicia.'

'I like you just the way you are, my friend.'

The fact that he claimed to like her...not her blue eyes or her fair skin, the things that were but a mask...gave her hope that, just perhaps, he saw her.

That their friendship was as genuine as it had ever been.

Thunder pounded, closer now. She imagined the storm was nearly on top of them. Rain pelted hard on the windows.

Breathe slowly, in and out, she told herself... focus on the conversation. Watch Will's mouth and pay attention to his words.

The library was safe...he had told her so. Seeing him unafraid made her feel somewhat steadier.

What had he been saying? Oh...yes, he asked if she was all right.

She nodded. 'It's just the storm that has me on edge. I'm quite fine really.'

If she kept on talking, he might not notice she was only nearly fine.

Besides, there was something she was intensely curious about.

It would be acceptable to ask since he had asked the same of her.

'Why haven't you married, Will? A man like you, so outgoing… I would think you would have by now.'

He shrugged, rolled his shoulders. 'I suppose I'm not the kind of man to take such a risk, if you want the truth. I saw what Phillip went through when he lost Cora and I suppose I do not have that much courage.'

It seemed an honest answer. But she wondered if that attitude would end up causing him unhappiness in the end. Phillip was the one to have suffered the loss and he was ready to take the risk and live again.

'But don't you fear being alone?' Surely he must. 'I cannot imagine living without a family of my own…but perhaps it is different for a man.'

'I couldn't say, since I've never been a woman.' What a tease he was, flashing those dimples at her.

'It's late, I should get back to my room.' She stood, not really wanting to go back, but it was past time she did.

He stood with her.

Suddenly the room blanched, stark and blazing white. An explosion of thunder shook everything, rumbling under her feet.

Oh, but then his arms were about her, holding her, patting her on the back and whispering that she was safe. Somehow, while he comforted her, his lips came close to hers...again. Unlike a few moments ago, she felt he was not going to resist kissing her.

She knew she was not going to resist kissing him.

For years she had daydreamed of this moment and now...well, his lips were a breath away. All she needed to do was lift up on her toes and his kiss would no longer be a dream.

He moved first, his mouth pressing briefly and, oh, so sweetly upon hers. And then, well... then she sighed.

To have her first kiss given to her by this man was...she did not know what for certain, but it was beyond wonderful.

She ought to say something, but she could not imagine what.

Will did know what to say. 'Welcome to Hawkwood.' He set her away from him, grinning playfully. 'I'm sorry. I should not have taken advantage of the moment.'

Not only did he know what to say, but, my word, the man knew how to kiss.

'Do you welcome all the ladies with a kiss?' She grabbed quick hold of her common sense. The last thing she wanted was to appear a maiden left witless.

Indeed not! She was woman full grown.

'Only ones who screech and throw themselves into my arms.'

'I did that? Then I do beg your pardon.' How could she have done something so embarrassing? 'I'll just be on my way again.'

With a nod and a devilishly dimpled grin he walked her to the door and opened it.

'Ginny...' he said softly when she passed by him.

'Yes?' Did she manage to make the word sound worldly-wise? Please do not let him guess she was agog over her first kiss.

'I...well, sweet dreams.'

'I wish you the same, Will.'

Now that did sound sophisticated, mature and casually stated.

She was under no illusion that this had been

anything but a simple flirtation on his part, but while she mounted the stairs to the second floor, she feared her dreams might be quite sweet and surely inappropriate.

There was every chance she would dream of the flirtatious smile of the Talton brother who did not wish to marry rather than the sober, yet sincere, smile of the one who did.

She must simply think of something else to occupy her mind, she decided while making her way back to her chamber.

Lady Kirkwynd's mischievous puppy seemed a safe place for her mind to dwell. While it was true that the considerate thing would have been to leave the dog at home, small Bernard was adorable. One could nearly overlook the fact that he chewed everything his mouth encountered.

'Ginny Penneyjons!' Her aunt's voice broke into her thoughts. 'What are you doing wandering the halls this time of night?'

Turning about, Ginny thought she might ask the same question of her aunt.

Adelia Monroe was not alone. Lord Helm stood beside her, his grey moustache lifting in a smile.

'I imagine the storm was keeping you awake,

my dear,' he said. 'The same as it was me and your aunt. With all the noise it is a wonder the entire household is not wandering the hallways.'

'Ginny never has been one for storms, have you, dear?'

She was not. However, her aunt was more like William in that she enjoyed the bluster.

'I would have knocked on your door, Auntie, but it appeared your lamp was out. I assumed you were asleep.'

'It was out, of course, since I had yet to retire to my room. Lord Helm and I were caught up in a game of chess and the time quite got away.' Her aunt smiled softly at her long-time friend. 'I only wish I had gone up sooner since you solidly trounced me.'

'It is a shame you did not come upon us sooner, Miss Ginny. We would have welcomed the company.'

Was that a wink her aunt just flashed her friend? Ginny had the distinct impression she had sent him some sort of message.

But it was dim in the hallway and the wink might have been no more than a common blink.

'Yes, it is a shame you were alone,' Aunt Adelia remarked. 'I hope you did not spend your time aimlessly wandering about.'

'In fact, I did not. I went to the library to get a book.'

'And you did not find one among them all to suit?' Aunt Adelia glanced at Ginny's empty hands.

'I forgot to look. Just as I was going in, Lady Talton's son was coming out. We ended up having a lovely chat.'

Lord Helm gave them each a nod. 'It is past time to put these old bones to bed. Thank you for staying up with me, Adelia. Your company was a welcome diversion.'

'Indeed, you might not say so to tomorrow. I invite you to another game in which I will trounce you roundly.'

'Ah, I do look forward to it,' he said, his smile at Aunt Adelia soft, affectionate. Then his attention shifted to include Ginny. 'Good night, ladies. Sleep well.'

'Shall I see you at breakfast?' Aunt Adelia asked.

'Oh, indeed you shall. This evening's game has left me with an appetite.'

For half a second she thought her aunt was

blushing, but again, it was dim in the hallway so she could not be certain.

'Tell me, Ginny, did you have a pleasant conversation with our host?' Given the time of night her aunt spoke quietly while they walked past closed chamber doors, some with lamplight seeping out from under the door, but more of them dark. 'It was quite clever of you to find a moment to be alone with him.'

'It was not at all clever, it was simply luck that we were in the same place at the same time.'

'Well, no matter. Any time you can spend with the Earl puts you ahead of the rest of the girls.'

'You make it sound like a race, Auntie. But at any rate it was not Phillip I spent time with, it was William.'

'Oh…was it, then? I hope you had a splendid time…but not too splendid, of course.'

'I imagine it was not nearly as splendid as your game of chess with Lord Helm.'

They had reached their rooms by now. Aunt Adelia kissed her cheek and wished her goodnight.

Ginny watched while her aunt closed her chamber door with a quiet click.

What was that? Laughter? Yes…her aunt was quite clearly chuckling.

It was a picture of a day here at the waterfall, warm, sunny and the sky crystal blue. William imagined poets visiting Ullswater were busily scribbling odes to it.

The last traces of last night's storm had blown away on a dawn breeze.

Recollections of last night had not.

Welcome to Hawkwood? Had he really uttered that inane comment to try to cover his blunder?

And blunder it was. What had got into him, kissing her like he had? Echoes of the past pulling at their heartstrings…taking them back to the children they had been…to a time they both dearly missed.

A token gesture to let each other know they cherished that moment out of time, nothing more.

It was as true now as it had been years ago. He liked her very much. He thought Phillip would be wise to give her a great deal of consideration.

And give it quickly, before William got sucked back into the past as he had last night. It had been a near miss, what with the storm and the intimacy of the cosy library. He had no intention of making a bid for Ginny's affections. Under no circumstances would he be disloyal to the brother he loved. Phillip's happiness meant everything to him.

More than his own? a sneaky voice in his mind suggested. Yes! His brother had been to hell and back. William would do nothing to jeopardise his recovery. Not only that, he would not do anything to ruin the friendship which had rekindled between him and Ginny.

All he could hope was that she had not been aware of his temporary loss of reason last night. From now on he would make sure to keep his thoughts firmly in the present, a present which was quite inviting just now.

Because of the fine weather many of Hawkwood's guests were attending the outing to Aira Force.

There were probably thirty of them gathered at the foot of the falls and gazing up. It didn't matter how often William stood at the pool below, the sight took his breath away.

Nearly seventy feet high, the fall spilled clear, sparkling water down a rocky, wooded chasm. A pair of rustic bridges crossed the fall, one at the top and one at the bottom.

The group was scheduled to dine al fresco in the glen above the falls. In his opinion it was one of the most picturesque spots in all of England.

If a man, if Phillip, was to fall in love, the glen would be the spot for it.

His mother, Aunt Adelia and Lord Helm stood beside the fence rail at the pool, gazing up for a time, but then turned away and walked towards the trail that led up to the glen.

'The woman has no shame,' he heard a voice whisper. He did not need to pivot about to know who the gossiper was... Lady Della.

'Who would wear such a thing to a picnic?' the lady—Jane, he thought it was—replied.

William stood where he was, gazing up at the fall, pretending not to hear them. For one, he had no wish to engage in the conversation and, for two, he wanted to know what else they would say.

'We can only be glad she did not bring that yappy dog along.' This from Lady Della.

'I've no doubt it would have chewed the shoes right off our feet.'

While the women did not approve of the way Lady Kirkwynd dressed, or of her tendency to bring the pup with her most places she went, he did not approve of their petty attitudes.

For all that they were bound to be jealous of the half-dozen young men gathered about the widow, admiring her as much as the falls, he suspected, it did not excuse their unkind words.

It was hard to imagine such petty talk going on when the beauty of Aira Force was all around.

They nattered on, the sound no more than a buzz until he heard his brother's name spoken in a resentful tone.

Following their gazes, he spotted Phillip laughing with Ginny and Lady Elizabeth.

In his opinion, Phillip did not look bored. Indeed, he looked the merriest that William had seen him in some time.

'Would you ladies care to accompany me to the glen?' This ought to put their busy mouths to rest for a while. 'I for one am getting hungry.'

'My goodness, that would be delightful, Mr Talton.' Lady Della was suddenly all smiles. Not because of his company, he figured, but because the closer they got to him, the better a chance they had to spend time with his brother.

'I imagine Lady Kirkwynd wishes she was with us.' Lady Della flicked her gaze at the object of her scorn. 'May I speak freely of something that has been a burden on my heart, Mr Talton? I would not spread gossip, you understand, but I care so very deeply for your brother and I would be crushed if he were hurt because I remained silent.'

Heaven help him... 'What is it, Lady Della?'

'It is only that I know things about the widow that you might not. If I may say so, she is unsavoury.'

'I have spent time with the lady. I have not found what you say to be true.'

Jane's mouth fell open, her chin bobbing up and down. 'But surely you have—'

He honestly had no interest in what Jane and Lady Della thought of the widow.

'Being such observant ladies, you must know a great deal about everyone. Tell me, what is your opinion of Lady Virginia, also of Lady Elizabeth.'

'I cannot say there is anything wrong with them, but you must have noticed they fail to shine,' Lady Della answered, looking for all the world as if she had just sucked on a lemon.

Strolling along the path, the girls chattered on, asking his advice on, of all things, what they should wear after dinner this evening. What would best please Phillip?

If he answered truthfully, he would tell them to don a charitable attitude. Whatever they put on over it did not matter.

'Lady Della, I have noticed that Mr Taylor seems to be smitten with you.'

'It is flattering, of course. He is very decent, but he is a second son.'

Perhaps, in their preoccupation with attracting his brother's attention, they had forgotten William was a second son. Were they truly oblivious that their flippant words degraded him, exposing attitudes that revealed he was unworthy in their eyes?

Never mind that. He did not feel unworthy. Probably because Phillip had never made him feel less...nor had his mother. Father had always made it known that William's value was as great as his brother's was, no matter that he was not Hawkwood's heir.

He was and had always been content to be Phillip's second in command. He was well suited to the job of second fiddle. The job which was, at the moment, to judge which lady was right for Phillip.

Naturally, he would have to say that neither Lady Della nor Jane was fit to be Countess. Either of those women would make his brother miserable.

But there were women here whom he thought were worthy of his brother's heart. Women he would rejoice to see become Lady Hawkwood.

Even if it was Ginny? There was that sneaky voice again. Especially if it was Ginny! He would gladly welcome her to the family.

For the rest of the walk up he ignored their nattering chat and focused his attention on lush green shrubs with flowers blooming among them.

Ah, just there…a harebell bobbed its lavender-blue head in greeting. He pointed it out, but the ladies gave it the barest glance. William bent to pick it. He tucked it into his shirt pocket.

He and the ladies were the first of the party to enter the glen.

Mother was busily directing the servants on the placement of blankets under the trees.

'Where will His Lordship sit?' Lady Della asked.

'I am sure I could not predict it. Ah, if you will excuse me, I must speak with my mother.'

He strode towards his mother, deciding if one of them called after him he would pretend not to hear.

'I am glad to see you, Mother, more than you know.' He kissed her cheek.

'I can but imagine.' She lowered her lids at his recent companions. 'Since you are here you may make yourself useful by keeping watch over our lunch. Shoo the squirrels away…and the flies as best you can.'

'I'll enjoy the company of wildlife invaders over those two,' he mumbled, but Mother had excellent hearing.

'Do not fret over them. They were not meant for your brother, anyway.'

What an odd thing to say. Had they not all come with an equal chance at Phillip?

'Is there someone who is meant for him?'

'But of course not! Just not the pair of them… or Lady Kirkwynd.'

'I find Lady Kirkwynd pleasant company… she is entertaining.'

'Is she? Well, as long as she entertains you and not your brother.'

She was right, of course. Lady Kirkwynd was

not for Phillip even they though they did have losing a spouse in common.

'Where are Aunt Adelia and Lord Helm? Did you not come up together?'

'Adelia took Lord Helm for a walk to Lyulph's Tower. I expect them in time for lunch. Oh, quick, William! There is a squirrel with his eye on the sandwiches.'

Hurrying towards the food table, he waved his arms and shouted. The small red creature scurried back up a tree. Looking down, it chattered at him.

Moments later he heard voices on the path. Phillip entered the shady glen escorting Ginny and Elizabeth, one lady on each arm.

In William's opinion Phillip and Elizabeth looked very well together. But to his mind, not as good as Phillip and Ginny did. Seeing the two of them enjoying each other's company was satisfying.

Ginny laughed quietly at something Phillip said.

All right, he felt satisfied and discontented at the same time. He had never had such an odd sensation settle in the pit of his stomach.

The truth of it was nothing would be better

than to welcome Ginny into the family. It would mean he would never have to say goodbye to her. But it would also mean—

He lost track of the thought because Ginny dropped Phillip's arm and made her way towards him, her smile warmer than the summer afternoon.

'I envy you,' Ginny said because it was the first thing that came to her mind when she joined William at the food table.

'For getting to chase off squirrels or swat flies?'

'For getting to live in this beautiful place. To have grown up with Aira Force so close by and the lake right outside your front door. I've always enjoyed the garden at Cliverton, but this is so much more.' She turned in a slow circle, breathing the air, looking at leafy trees growing in the grassy meadow…sealing the beauty of it in her heart for the day she would have to go home.

A pair of servants walked up to the table to relieve William of his watch.

'I nearly had a squirrel by its tail, but it was a quick rascal,' he told the kitchen girls with a teasing wink.

'Did you really?' Ginny asked while he led her towards the blanket where Phillip and Elizabeth sat.

'It's true! Had I been half a second quicker I'd be presenting you with a pet.'

'One cannot keep a squirrel as a pet.'

She sat down on the blanket in the space next to Phillip. William took the spot on the other side of her. Being flanked by Taltons was rather nice. She was becoming fond of them both and quite rapidly.

Of course, she had always been fond of the boy Will. Now here was the man she was only now getting to know. Oddly though, in some ways, it felt as though she had never ceased knowing him.

Now that she was reacquainted with him, she was not certain how it made her feel. Happy, of course, since she had only dreamed of seeing William again. Troubled, too, though. It would not be long before she went home and she feared she would miss the man even more than she had the boy.

There was only one way she would remain at Hawkwood and that was to wed the Earl.

And here she sat between the brothers, so unlike each other and yet endearing for their differences.

As confusing as it was, she could not imagine anything more pleasant than spending a warm afternoon in this beautiful spot.

'It's what I told William about squirrels,' Phillip said with a quick nod at his brother. 'Found out I was wrong.'

'It is possible to do, but not easy.' Will's smile was so different from his brother's. Phillip's was warm and engaging, Will's bright and teasing. 'The trick is, you need to raise it from a kit. Then when the time comes, after it is nearly grown, you've got to be able to let it go. Mother will be the first to tell you they need trees to climb and not curtains.'

Ginny heard a murmur of voices, laughing and chatting as a group from below neared the glen.

'But did it still know you...afterwards?'

'I like to think she did, but whenever I went out and called for her I brought her favourite snack...so it could be that she scampered across the grass for the cracker and not for me.'

She liked that about Will...that he had kept a squirrel. It was touching to imagine him as a little boy holding the creature, probably petting it and kissing its soft red head.

Lost in the image, smiling over it, she failed to notice Lady Della take a spot on the blanket.

At once she commandeered the conversation, making certain Phillip's attention was focused solely on her.

Naturally Elizabeth appeared less than pleased since Lady Della had squeezed into the spot between her and Phillip, forcing her to move over. Not only that, whenever Elizabeth tried to speak, Lady Della spoke over her.

'I wonder where Lady Kirkwynd is,' Will whispered. He needn't have whispered since the two of them were clearly as left out of the conversation as Elizabeth was.

Looking past Will's shoulder, she saw the widow glancing about at the people taking places on blankets.

'Over there,' Ginny pointed out.

There was something in the widow's glance— it was fleeting, but Ginny recognised it. Where would she sit? Which group of strangers would welcome her?

How startling to discover a lady of such apparent self-confidence could be unsure of her reception.

Will stood up. Waving his arm, he invited her over.

Lady Kirkwynd smiled, laughed in that way she had, caught her red skirt in a bright swish, then made her way over.

There was not much room on the blanket so Will moved over to the grass, giving his spot to her. With so many people now chatting, or attempting to, Ginny was happy that Will's new spot brought him closer to her than he had been before.

There was no reason it should bother her that Will singled out Lady Kirkwynd to join them. Whether the invitation was out of kindness or because he fancied her was really no business of Ginny's.

Besides, like every other lady here, the woman was here to get to know Phillip.

Wasn't it odd that the thought of Lady Kirkwynd getting to know the Earl did not trouble her one little bit, but the thought of her getting to know Will…well, it felt rather distressing?

She must bear in mind that Will was her friend

and nothing more. Lady Kirkwynd had as much right to his friendship as anyone did.

Indeed, she was only grateful to have had the chance to rekindle her acquaintance with Will. She was reminded that back then, there had been more than common friendliness between them. The attachment they formed went quite deep for all that they had only spent an afternoon and evening together.

Looking at him now, a man with summer sunshine in his hair, and his smile so...well, it just touched her in a way that made her feel she could sit here all day and smile back at him.

She did wonder what exactly she was hoping to rekindle.

Never mind. There was friendship between them now so she meant to enjoy these moments.

'Tell me, Will, did you keep the squirrel under the bed with the fawn?' she had to ask.

'The fawn came first. A few months later, the squirrel.' He tipped his head, flashing his dimples. 'The duck came the year after.'

'You had a duck! Was it under your bed? How green with envy do I look?'

He touched her chin, turning her face this way and that. Something inside her shivered which was odd since his fingers on her skin felt… spicy? Indeed, spicy nicely described the sensation. She was only dimly aware of guests walking past with food.

'Yes… I see it, green just there at the corners of your mouth.' Where was her breath? Her heart suffered no such lapse, it galloped against her ribs because…well those spicy fingers were so close to her lips and any second now someone was bound to notice he was touching her chin. 'Definitely green, but not as bright as grass, more like moss.'

'He didn't have it long, Lady Ginny.'

Oh, she had not been aware that Phillip was paying attention to the conversation.

'Mother made me return it to the lake when she heard it quacking under my bed.'

'A fowl is foul no matter where it is,' Lady Della inserted, laughing and probably hoping the Earl found her remark as witty as she did.

'Do you dislike them on the dinner table, Lady Della?' Lady Kirkwynd asked, one slim dark brow arched in question. 'I got the impression last night you were rather fond of duck.'

The colour rose in Lady Della's cheeks, bright red and flaming.

'Lady Virginia, would you care to walk with me for a few moments?' Phillip asked.

'Oh, yes, my lord. A walk would be just the thing.'

She should not let it, but her mind shot back to the day when Will asked her the same thing. The flash of mischief in his eyes as they dashed away from the rest of the group was as clear in memory as it had been on the afternoon it happened.

Lord Hawkwood's invitation was a welcome one. A diversion was exactly what she needed.

Not only to get away from the tension between the three women, but a moment to settle her heart after Will's touch.

'You will keep the ladies amused while I am gone?' Phillip asked his brother.

William smiled, but Ginny noticed the humour usually brightening his expression was dimmed.

And no wonder. The last thing anyone would want was to have to amuse that trio of pecking hens. She only hoped Elizabeth had a sharp enough beak to hold her own.

There was a path beside a stream which fed Aira Force. Phillip led her along it.

'I'm sorry to draw you away, Ginny. I hope

you do not mind terribly. It's only that if I heard one more cackle… I do beg your pardon, that was not a gentlemanly comment.'

'You needn't guard your thoughts around me. Speaking candidly is so refreshing. Besides, I agree, one more word would have been a bit much to take.'

It was peaceful here with water gurgling swiftly past and small birds twittering about in branches arching overhead.

'How do you find Hawkwood, Ginny? Comfortable, I hope.'

'It might be the loveliest place I have ever visited. I will miss the fresh air and blue skies when Aunt Adelia and I return to London. Not to mention missing a view of Lake Ullswater from my chamber window. I believe I could sit there all day, just watching sunshine glitter off the water and the *Raven* paddling by with tourists waving greetings from the deck.'

'I know what you mean. All the while I am in London I think of home. I enjoy London, do not mistake me, but one does not find the peace there that one does here.'

'Indeed, and you will not find a waterfall like Aira Force close by, either. You and William were fortunate to have grown up here.' She glanced sideways at him, met his easy smile with one of her own. 'But I must say it was a lucky thing you yanked him out of the barrel when you did. William told me about some of the mischief you caught him at.'

'Mostly I kept quiet about it, but when he tried to go over the falls? Naturally, I had to speak up. Father gave him a good blistering for it. I am surprised he told you about that. It was not his proudest moment and I do not believe he has admitted it to anyone.'

Hadn't he? Now that made her feel rather grand, in a fuzzy sort of way. Perhaps her friendship with Will was as special to him as it was to her.

Perhaps over the years, he had carried the memory of their day together as close to his heart as she had. The thought made her want to go skipping along the path.

Had she been alone she might have done just that.

She and Phillip walked in comfortable silence for a time, listening to small rustlings in the brush and laughter reaching from the picnic area.

'Tell me, Ginny, what do you think of my brother?'

'Well, he is brave. You would not have left him with the ladies if it were not true.'

'But he is fond of women so entertaining them is a pleasure more than a chore.'

'In most cases, maybe. But to be left alone with Lady Della and Lady Kirkwynd... I think he is heroic.' She laughed, wondering if William had been forced to banish anyone to a different blanket yet. 'You owe him a debt...he has told me as much.'

'Did he mention how I might repay it, for it is true that I do.'

'He is going to ask you for a horse who will best yours in a race, I believe, when he gets the chance.'

'He told you we enjoy racing? Mother is not aware of it, by the way.'

'I'll keep your secret.'

'That is two secrets of mine you now hold. I believe we are bound in some way.' His laugh was as congenial as his smile. 'Did my brother ever mention that he allowed me to beat him in a race?'

'He might have…yes. But he also vows he will not let you do it again.'

'I was not myself then, due to losing Cora.' He was silent for a moment. 'But I am ready to wed again. You need have no concern about that.'

Why, she wondered, had he wanted to point it out? Did he confess this to every lady he spent time with or was the admission meant for her especially?

Could this admission mean he was considering her more seriously than some of the other ladies? She ought to be thrilled, of course. She did like Phillip a great deal even though they were only just getting to know one another.

Naturally, she was not going to ask.

'My brother speaks freely with you, I think.'

'I'm certain he speaks freely with all the ladies. I suspect it is in his nature to do so.'

Phillip nodded, looking at her in a way she could not read.

'Will and I have always got along, though. Even when we were children,' she said. 'And even though it was only the one day.'

'Well then, you are the very one to deliver a message from me.'

'Yes…all right. You may count upon me.'

'Tell him that I do not owe him a faster horse than the one I have.' In the instant, Phillip's smile was as full of zest as Will's always was. 'Because, losing a race is the last thing I intend to do.'

Chapter Seven

William sat bolt upright in bed, visions from a nightmare still twisting his emotions.

Getting up, he lit a lamp, then strode to the window to gaze at Hawkwood's pasturelands, at fells grazed in moonlight rising rugged beyond them.

He pushed open the window, hoping for a rush of fresh air to wash away the odd and disturbing images lingering in his mind.

The events of the dream were twisted, places and people made little sense. Even as he tried to recall them, the details faded.

There had been a wedding... Ginny's... and Phillip's. In the dream they were leaving Hawkwood in a carriage, Ginny in her wedding gown...her hair was loose, flying about as if it were windy, although no one else was touched by the gust. Her fair strands covered Phillip's face, blocking his eyes from William's view, but his mouth was visible. Phillip was grinning broadly...wait...he did it with half a mouth! The image was grotesque. How could his brain have imagined such a thing?

Slower to fade than the distressing images was his gut-tearing desperation to catch up with the coach. People milling about the yard seemed untroubled by the coach's departure. It was as if they existed apart from him and the carriage. His feet were stuck in mud and no one to help him get free. He screamed Ginny's name over and over. It was the screaming which awakened him.

Hang it, but he could not recall ever feeling more relief to wake from a bad dream. He'd had a conviction of such dread that if the carriage left Hawkwood, something life changing...something wicked would happen.

It was not clear to whom the wicked thing would happen...to Ginny...to Phillip...or to him? Or perhaps all three of them.

He took a deep breath of brisk air and let it out slowly. The leftover impression of separation, of intense grief, began to fade.

Now, with his heart slowing, his emotions settling, he let the nightmare go. Perhaps he'd had too much dessert after dinner tonight and that was the simple cause of it.

All was well. Wide awake, he felt what he always did when he looked out this window… contentment…a sense of well-being that went bone deep.

Cake was at the heart of the troubled dream and nothing more. Certainly not a warning that Ginny wedding his brother would be a great disaster…for William.

Dreams! He would be glad when he could laugh at this bizarre one.

It was cooler outside than he expected. Rather than close the window he reached for the shirt he had worn today. It was easily at hand because it was his habit before sleeping to gaze at the stars, to remove his shirt and feel fresh air off Lake Ullswater wash away the day.

When he shrugged into the sleeves, the flower he had picked earlier in the day fell out of the pocket.

He stooped to pick it up. It was a pretty thing, even if half-wilted. Twirling it between his finger and thumb, he was reminded of why he had plucked it.

He had meant to give it to Ginny, to place it in her hair and admire the way the lavender-blue shade of the petals matched her eyes.

It was what he had intended, but then Phillip had snatched her away and he hadn't had the chance.

Which was probably for the best. He did not wish to give Ginny an incorrect impression of his feelings towards her. Giving flowers was a thing a man did when he was courting a lady. Which he was not doing. And if he were courting a lady it would not be his brother's lady.

The dream image of Phillip's half-smile disturbed him. Even though the vision had been caused by an excess of cake, it did haunt him.

He closed the window, going back to his bed.

Surely daylight would rout the lingering disquiet.

Ginny tapped her fingers on the cover of her journal where it lay on the writing desk in her chamber. It had been some time since she had opened it.

She did not miss the characters she had written with such devotion, but she did miss writing.

If she opened the pages and read those words,

she would probably be embarrassed by it. For a time, those improbable stories had served a purpose, perhaps helped to fill the void left by her parents' deaths and the shyness which had become worse after losing Mama. Not to mention writing them had helped to keep the object of her first and only crush alive in her heart.

She was ready now to pick up her pen.

But not to record the latest gossip or social trends as Will once guessed she was writing. Why write sordid things when there was a beautiful world beyond her chamber window waiting to be put to words?

What better time than now to begin? Her hosts had not made plans for the afternoon. Phillip had announced that today was to be spent unstructured since he had estate business to attend to.

She imagined Will was glad for the time off, as well.

Guests were free to visit the towns scattered around Lake Ullswater or even take a walking tour of it. Or to remain at Hawkwood, stroll the gardens or nap under shady trees. From her window she spotted Lord Helm doing just that, his feet crossed at the ankle and his hands resting over his chest.

Well then, she knew exactly what she would do.

Gathering up her writing supplies, she went happily down the stairway, out the front door and into the fresh, sunny day.

The view from the porch easily took one's breath away. She stood for a moment, looking at the swathe of lawn stretching from the front of the house to the lake where a wooden dock stood, its glittering image reflected in water.

There were benches set about so that one might sit and enjoy the beauty. Some of them were in the shade and some in sunshine. Some of them lined paths bordered with flowers and others were half hidden in secluded spots.

Since she wished for both privacy and a view of what she wished to write about, she chose a bench under a shady tree where she could see what went on, but was not likely to be interrupted. It was going to take a great deal of concentration to paint the flowers and the sky with precise and pretty words.

Oh, but it was lovely and quiet with so many of the guests away for the afternoon.

The sky—she would begin describing the purest blue she had ever seen. She nearly began to write that it was a match to Will's eyes, but, no…

she was no longer writing about people, real or imagined.

'Stop!'

That drew her attention away from the search for a perfect adjective.

Looking up, she spotted Lady Kirkwynd chasing after her puppy who was merrily scampering across the lawn with a hat, its blue satin ribbons flapping merrily behind.

The Baroness stopped running. Breathing hard, she slammed her hands on her hips and glared, horrified, at the pup. And no wonder. Little Bernard also took that moment to stop... to shake the hat and then shred it.

Hopefully the ruined bonnet belonged to Lady Kirkwynd, otherwise some lady was going to be quite unhappy.

What was her first name? Ginny wondered. Did anyone know it? For as outgoing as she was, the widow was also quite private.

Ginny focused her attention back to the word she had been in search of.

Blue, was it not? The colour of Will's eyes... no, not that. Of course, she meant the sky.

And if she were writing about the colour of

eyes she would be describing how Phillip's eyes were a lovely brown shade of—

Glancing about, she did not see anything the shade of Lord Hawkwood's eyes.

Perhaps it would be best to write about flowers. A pretty bunch of them bobbed their delicate orange heads only feet from where she sat. Since they were not the colour of anyone's eyes the description should be quite straightforward.

'You scamp.' Glancing up yet again, Ginny watched Lady Kirkwynd pry the ruined hat from Bernard.

Walking towards the house, she nuzzled her nose in Bernard's fur.

'Sweetly scented posies' she scratched across the page.

Someone screeched.

Ah, it was Lady Della who had lost the hat.

'You little beast!'

It looked as though Lady Della reached for the puppy, but Lady Kirkwynd shoved the ruined hat into her hands. 'Mother will be furious!'

Ginny refocused her attention on describing how when sunshine grazed flower petals, they shimmered. One had to look closely to see it, but the sight was more than a little magical.

The weight of the bench shifted. Lady Della sat down beside her with a heavy plonk. Drat it! Ginny could feel the heat of her outrage while she yanked on the frayed blue ribbons, flicking a finger at the chewed brim.

'There will be a price to be paid for this,' she muttered.

Ginny wondered who would pay it—Lady Kirkwynd, the pup, or Lady Della when her mother discovered the ruined hat?

'Puppies do chew.' It was a shame about the hat, but really, who could truly resent a sweet and adorable puppy?

'Why would anyone want one of the beasts?'

'Because they are loving little beasts.'

Lady Della huffed…snorted, really, but she breathed deeply, evidently trying to calm herself.

Dark clouds slid across the tops of the fells. A breeze blew in off the lake, fluttering the pages of the journal.

The crisp snap caught Lady Della's attention. Her sharp, curious gaze fell upon it.

'What are you writing? Perhaps something witty to distract me from my ordeal?'

'You would not find it entertaining. I am simply writing descriptions of flowers and sky, that's all.'

'Let me see… I'm certain I saw something… Justina, was it… Admirable?' Lady Della reached for the journal. 'Surely that is more interesting than flowers.'

She pressed the journal close to her chest. If Lady Della got a hold of her journal, read the adventures which were meant for no eyes but her own…well, she might never get over the humiliation.

'It looks as though rain is coming. You would not want to explain a wet gown as well as the ruined bonnet to your mother.'

'Perhaps you will show me your journal another time, then.' Lady Della stood, shook the hat and frowned at it. 'I will need distraction even more once I face Mother's scolding over this.'

Lady Della hurried across the lawn towards the house even though there was probably still a bit of time before the rain began to fall.

With the peace of the afternoon ruined, and creativity fled from her brain, Ginny decided to take a walk along the shoreline while there was still time.

* * *

From where he sat in the shade of a great tree, William watched shifting shades of blue play across the surface of Lake Ullswater. This moment of tranquillity was beyond price. It felt wonderful to do nothing more than keep his mouth shut, not have to think of what to say to keep anyone entertained.

Lying back with his head cradled in his hands, he gazed up into the leafy canopy and let his mind go still.

Peace…beautiful…blessed quiet.

A woman screeched.

Before the screech ended, he was on his feet.

Ah, it was Lady Della Robinn. Seeing her marching away from Lady Kirkwynd, he sat back down.

Of all the ladies in attendance, it was those two who were most at odds.

Gazing up at the leaves shifting and whispering in the light wind, he decided to leave whatever it was to be handled between them.

Hearing footsteps, he looked towards the sound.

Ginny! What a relief to see it was her.

'I heard Lady Della screech. Is there trouble?' Oh, please do not let there be trouble.

'Oh, well, yes.' But it could not be horrible trouble because her eyes sparkled—mischievously, in his opinion. 'It might come to it in the end.'

'Let's walk out on the dock and you can tell me about it.'

The dock was not long, only about forty feet, but it was half as wide. He and Phillip used to dive into the lake from it. William still did so late at night when the weather was warm enough and the household abed.

'Please, tell me what tragedy has beset us.'

Her lips twitched...he was fairly sure his heart did, too.

'Bernard chewed Lady Della's hat.' Ginny laughed quietly, covering her mouth and shaking her head. 'Thoroughly destroyed it.'

The sound went through him, straight to his funny bone...or wherever one's sense of frolic was located. He began to laugh with her even though he had no idea why a ruined hat was cause for humour.

She took a deep breath, pressing her hand to her middle.

'I do not know why we are laughing,' he said, although it felt wonderful to be doing so.

It was interesting how laughter came so easily between them. The only other person he had ever experienced this sort of thing with was Phillip.

'Oh, well, it isn't really. But the pup seemed so proud of his prize and Lady Della...but you are correct, it isn't funny...not terribly at least.'

Out on the dock the breeze was stronger, cooler with a ribbon of inky clouds skimming the tops of the fells. As pretty as the weather now was, those clouds did indicate a change on the way. It could be raining sooner than he would like.

'Not so terribly...but I would like to have seen it. Everyone enjoys a happy pup, don't they?'

She touched his arm where he had rolled back his sleeves. It felt the most natural thing in the world, her fingers on his arm...so friendly and... and amicable. But since when had an amicable touch shot heat all through him?

Never was when.

'I would like to see what happens when she confronts her mother...oh—' She covered her mouth with her fair, pretty hand. 'That was not a well-mannered thing to say. I do beg your pardon.'

'Let's sit down on the dock and think of other ill-mannered things to talk about.'

They did sit, swinging their legs as if they were once again carefree children, although they did not waste time talking about other people.

What was it between them that made being together feel so natural?

Theirs was no common friendship and make no mistake about it.

They were not in love and could not be even if... Of course there was no even if, so he put it from his mind.

'Here comes the *Raven*.' Ginny lifted her arm to wave and several people on the boat waved back. 'I'll miss that when I go back to London. If you wave to strangers in passing carriages, you will get odd looks.'

'What if you do not go back?' Indeed, what if she did not? It would mean he would get to see her every day and that would be wonderful...but he would see her as his brother's wife. It gave his insides the queerest feeling. Having Ginny as a sister? Would it feel right? In his dream it had been anything but right. 'Would you refuse my brother if he asked for your hand?'

'I would ask for some time to consider it. Such a decision is not one of a moment. Unless you happen to be my sister, Felicia, then it is. She decided to wed quite quickly.'

'But I understand it worked out rather well for her.'

'She is blissfully happy. She lives close by, in Windermere.'

'Yes, I have heard. We should go to visit one day.'

'I'd have done so before now, but she and her husband are travelling.'

Asking Ginny to go visiting had not been appropriate since it should be Phillip asking that. He had overstepped and would be careful not to do so again.

Besides, suggesting a visit had been a casual remark more than anything.

What he wanted to say was of a far different nature. Until he asked, he would not know.

'But, Ginny, would you consider my brother's suit? Do the two of you get along well enough?'

As well as the two of them did? As well as

sugar and spice, salt and pepper…birds and bees? No, not that last.

'I think we do. Your brother is an easy man to get along with,' she said, her brows dipping to a delicate frown.

What was she thinking…feeling? The question had been forward and he probably should not have probed her intentions that way.

It was none of his business…except that Phillip was his business. But had he presented the question for the sake of his brother, or for his own sake? And what did he even mean, for his own sake? Nothing was what!

Ginny had come here to explore a life with Phillip.

To his relief, she smiled, then shrugged. He cast his twisted thoughts to the rising wind, letting them blow away across the lake.

They got along fine as friends and so they would remain.

'What I fear…' She did not say what at first, but simply looked at him, into his eyes in a way that— '…is that he will not consider me an appropriate choice as Countess once I dance with him at the ball. I've not an ounce of grace and it is a skill a countess ought to have. Do not be surprised if I come down with some mysterious ailment and am forced to miss the ball.'

He stood up, reaching a hand down to her.

'Come, I will teach you to dance.'

'Now? Here?'

'I promise not to spin you into the water.'

'The promise I need is that you will not push me in after I stomp on your big toe.'

'I'll fish you out if I do.'

She smiled, with her pretty pink mouth, with her sparkling eyes. Reaching up, she clasped his hand.

Poor Will.

His smile was bright, confident. Too soon it was bound to become a frown.

How long until he discovered his attempt was futile? She was not graceful, he could not transform her.

Her dancing instructors had given up in despair long ago.

Oh, but Will looked so hopeful. She would do her best not to let him down.

'Just follow me, count along to the time of one,

two, three. When there is music it will feel natural and you will no longer need to count.'

'Feel free to give up on me at any time. I will not be offended.'

'Nonsense. Anyone can dance.'

Oh, yes, poor Will. Rather than argue the point she would let him discover the truth for himself.

'You know how to begin, I'm certain. You place your hand on my arm…up close to my shoulder.' He lifted her hand and placed it there. Then he cupped his hand at the small of her back, took her free hand and held the pose.

For mercy's sake! Did he truly think she would be able to count out steps when his hand pressed so big and firm on her back? She had no way of knowing if her hand would feel so sparkling, so titillating nestled in another man's hand. She rather thought not.

If this was all there was to dancing, she could do it all day and night. Of course, they had yet to move. Clouds were quickly covering the sun. With any luck it would begin to rain before she disgraced herself.

'Are you ready?' He looked confident of success.

'One, two, three,' she answered with a sigh.

'One.' He stepped back, drawing her forward with gentle pressure on her back. No doubt he expected that she would gracefully flow along after him. Her step was stiff. 'Two…feet together now.'

The toe of her shoe caught on an uneven plank. She stumbled, he righted her.

'Now, on three, a gliding step towards the side.'

She had seen this done, admired the way people made it look so easy. Sadly, when she attempted a graceful glide she stepped on his foot and the glide turned into a near fall.

This was so embarrassing. She had, however, warned him.

It was a good thing Will was strong and patient.

Setting her to rights again, he maintained his smile. If he was shocked by her clumsiness, he hid it well.

'The thing to keep in mind is that the gentleman leads and the lady follows. Relax, try to not resist my lead and this will be as natural as breathing.'

Except that feeling the warmth of his firm hold

upon her in the dance pose made her wonder if she was, in fact, breathing.

Even if she was, her bones had dissolved and she could not feel her feet.

Feet which were supposed to carry her gracefully about.

'Now back the other way.'

'Don't forget about fishing me out of the water.'

He laughed and she felt joy ripple from heart to knees to toes.

Perhaps she would manage the next set of one, two, three. But even if she did manage the count, what came after was a turn. She had every confidence a spin would not end well.

'I think I felt a raindrop,' she said.

'I like rain.'

'Yes, but—'

'One, two, three.'

The gentle pressure at her back drew her in the direction she was supposed to go which now had her stepping backwards.

Well, that was odd. Somehow, going backwards felt easier. Or was it that she was looking into Will's eyes and forgetting to worry about her feet?

'Better,' he announced, his grin wide with approval.

Wind came up, rushing along the deck planks and yanking her skirt about her legs, streaking his hair across his forehead.

'Again.'

One, two, three.

Her foot stomped down on his toe.

He grunted. She groaned.

'It's all right, Ginny. It needs practice, that's all.'

A smattering of raindrops slapped her head.

'It appears we have run out of time for practice.'

'Twirl,' he said in answer, then spun her about.

This time she stepped on her own toe, caught his shirt front to steady herself.

Rain dripped down his face. Glistening drops settled in his dimples, pooled at the corners of his mouth.

'We are getting wet,' she pointed out.

He touched her cheek, swiped moisture off her nose with a sweep of his thumb.

'Do you mind?'

Mind? Show her the woman who would mind?

She would need to get a great deal wetter than this to step away from the big bold hand still cupping her waist.

'It seems to rain quite often here.' Which would account for how green and lovely everything was. 'But, Will, you must admit I will not become an accomplished dancer before the ball.'

He stepped closer, shielding her from wet gusts, in as much as he could.

'You're frightened,' he said.

'I do not like being the centre of attention.'

'Of the storm, I mean.'

'I do not mind a bit of rain as long as it does not thunder.'

'I think you might be right about the dancing… not that I have conceded defeat. There will be other lessons. When you dance with my brother you will glide along with the best of them. But for now, let's get out of the weather.'

'The ball is in three days. You must not hold out hope of it.'

Even with rain dripping on him, Will did not lose a smidgen of good humour.

Looking towards the house as they dashed along the dock, she spotted Phillip standing under the portico of the porch.

He watched them run through the rain for a moment, then raised his arm, gesturing for them to hurry inside.

'I wonder how long he was watching,' Will said. 'Wouldn't want him to guess our secret.'

Chapter Eight

A game of croquet was the scheduled activity for the afternoon.

Listening to the click of mallets hitting balls, William came down the front steps.

It was a colourful sight, the ladies in their gowns chatting and playing.

There was his mother, leaning on her mallet while speaking with Aunt Adelia and Lord Helm.

Even if the country party did not end with a match for Phillip, at least Mother and her friends would have had a fine time.

But there would be matches, he was certain of it. Romance was in the air for at least three pairs of guests playing croquet.

Some of the guests gathered on the dock, waiting for the *Raven* to chug past. It had become an event, encouraging the pilot to blow the boat's whistle. Most of the time he did.

Lady Della was among those waiting on the dock. So was Lady Kirkwynd, her toothy pup clutched under her arm.

They stood side by side and as far as he could tell they appeared cordial with one another. However, appearances could be deceiving. In his opinion Lady Della was not one to quickly forget a perceived wrong done to her.

Ginny and Elizabeth stood at the shoreline involved in a chat.

As she typically did, Ginny stood out from among the others. Today she wore a blue gown and an ivory-coloured hat. Unless he was mistaken, and he could be given she was a fair distance away, but it appeared that she had tucked roses into the hat brim.

He stared harder. Yes, she had and they were the same variety as the ones he had given her at the train station. Funny how it made him feel all smiley inside.

What had prompted her to decorate the bonnet with them? Did she think of him when she placed them there?

More likely she had done it because they were pretty flowers. He should not think too much of it.

Chances are she put them there to please Phillip. His brother was a lucky man to have such a lady seeking his attention.

William, being the devoted brother he was and being the dear friend he was, was going to do what he could to make sure she got it.

Everyone seemed to be getting on, keeping entertained without his help. Perhaps it would be possible to sneak away with Ginny for another dance lesson.

It was true that she needed a great deal of practice. The ball was two days from now. He meant to make certain she had no hesitation in dancing with Phillip. If he could manage it, she would waltz about the ballroom in his brother's arms as effortlessly as any other lady.

He would stand at the edge of the dance floor and watch with a confident smile. He would feel as proud as a peacock.

Phillip and Ginny…what a brilliant couple they would be.

The thought made him want to weep…with joy.

The thrum of the *Raven*'s engine announced it was about to pass by the dock.

Guests on the dock began to wave. Even those playing croquet stopped their game to join in.

The pilot blew the whistle.

Lady Della jumped up, clapped her hands. The movement shifted her hip to the right, bumping Lady Kirkwynd, who fell sideways into the water.

Luckily, the point where she went in was only chest deep. She would be able to wade back to shore.

Would be, had she not lost hold of Bernard. The pup swam towards deeper water. The Baroness went after him.

'Stop!' he shouted on a run.

The floor of the lake fell away suddenly. With her skirts weighted down by water she would sink.

She must not have heard him because she kept on. He would not reach her in time.

Ginny, hearing his shout, turned to look at him. She must have read the alarm in his expression because she tugged on Elizabeth's sleeve.

Side by side they waded into the lake.

His heart went dead cold. None of the ladies were aware that the lake floor dropped away. He ran, an urgent prayer on his lips that they would stop Lady Kirkwynd before reaching that point.

Blame it! That point was only ten feet out from where they were.

'Stop!' he shouted, but they would not hear him over the boat's long, deep whistle and the chug of the engine.

There! Ginny caught Lady Kirkwynd's elbow. A second later Elizabeth snagged her shoulder.

The Baroness pointed frantically towards the puppy. She resisted being pulled back towards the shore.

William ripped off his coat while he ran. Took half a second to yank his shoes off.

Charging off the end of the dock, he dived into the water. He surfaced several feet from the pup. Seeing him, Bernard changed direction and paddled towards him.

He tucked the pup in the crook of his arm, then side-paddled to a spot where he could stand. He waded out of the lake, his heart pounding harder than it had ever done.

People laughed and cheered, not understanding what a disaster this might have been.

Phillip must have come out of the house just

in time to see what happened. His expression looked as alarmed as William had ever seen it.

Wading into shallower water with Bernard clutched in his arms, he watched Phillip stride quickly across the grass.

His brother's frown was justified. William would not be surprised if Phillip forbade anyone to go on to the dock. This accident could have been a fatal one.

If it even was an accident. He would not want to unduly accuse Lady Della of wrongdoing... but she did bear ill will towards Lady Kirkwynd and her pup.

Once on shore, the Baroness rushed for him. She plucked Bernard from his arms, buried her face in his sodden fur. He thought she was quietly weeping, but her face was so wet he could not determine if the moisture was tears or lake water.

Bernard, as puppies will, wagged his tail madly.

Without speaking, the Baroness turned to Ginny, gave her a great hug and then did the same to Elizabeth.

Completely soaked she ran for the house. She stopped at the foot of the steps, made a quick turn, then walked around the corner of the house.

This woman was not who people thought she was, he was certain of it. The lady she portrayed herself to be would take the shortest way into the house with no care for getting water on the fine wood floors. By going in the back door she would be dripping on stone and no harm done.

'May I have your attention?' He looked up to see Phillip walking to the point on the deck where the water got deeper.

He needn't have asked for their attention since everyone was already gathered about the dock, probably wondering why their host was so distraught over the incident.

'The accident you just witnessed was far more dangerous than you realise.'

William glanced at Ginny in the same instant she looked at him. She, too, must suspect the casual bump might not have been accidental.

'I would ask you all to be careful while on the dock. Pay attention to where I am standing.' He pointed at the deck, then the lake. 'The lake floor falls away suddenly. Lady Kirkwynd missed catastrophe by only a few feet. I do urge you all to be cautious.'

Clearly not in a mood to socialise, he strode

off the dock and followed his soaking guest towards the back of the house.

Always the responsible one, the Earl would see to Lady Kirkwynd's well-being before joining the rest of the group.

William walked towards Ginny and Elizabeth. Now that everyone was safe, he could appreciate the situation...smile at the way ruined hairdos sagged, dripping on slumped shoulders...to indulge in a grin at the way they swiped water from their faces.

He figured Ginny would not mind it if he laughed out loud. Indeed, she would laugh with him.

Elizabeth, though—he wondered if she would take the dousing more seriously.

Apparently, he was not going to discover the truth of it because Elizabeth's mother whisked her away.

'Don't laugh at me.' Ginny spoke through a hank of hair crossing her mouth. 'Don't you dare.'

But he did dare because she did it first.

'I'll walk you back to the house,' he said.

'You had better retrieve your shoes first.'

A moment later he was back at her side, his dry

coat slung over his shoulder, his wet feet making squelching sounds in his shoes.

She placed her hand in the crook of his arm. 'We must look a sight. As if we are indulging in an afternoon stroll looking like a pair of...well, I cannot think of what.'

'Not as good as ducks.' Glancing sidelong at her, he thought he could fall in love with a woman who could recover from a soaking with such good humour. Not this woman...of course. But one identical to her. As if such a woman existed. 'Water rolls right off them.'

He must remember, she was not, nor would she ever be, meant for him...not in the way she was meant for Phillip. At least, if her brother did choose her, she would remain in his life.

That was something to be glad for. Having been reunited with his childhood friend, he could not imagine being separated from her.

'Hmmm, but I do feel rather like I am waddling with all this weight.'

'Quack,' he blurted.

'Quack,' she answered back.

Right then he knew it. He would never find a woman like Ginny Penneyjons.

What was the point of even trying to?

'Well then, Will, what do you think?'

He thought he would be glad if she chose Phillip so that she would remain in his life.

If he could not love her as…no, he would not allow himself to think of it. But he could think of loving her as a sister.

He could do that and be grateful for it. To consider anything else led only to heartache. That was one road he would not travel.

He did not dare to wonder what would happen if Phillip did not choose Ginny. He shied away from the idea before it fully formed because even that much was a betrayal of his brother.

If there was one person he would not betray, it was his big brother…the one who had already suffered so much. The one who, even in the depth of his grief, had not betrayed everyone who depended upon him by failing in his duty to Hawkwood.

He must have been silent for too long because she added, 'Was the bump an accident? I saw it and I'm not certain.'

'Nor am I, but at least no one was injured. Praise the Good Lord for it, because a few more feet and it might have ended very differently.'

'Perhaps Lady Kirkwynd will know. Although

I do not see how she could since one moment she was waving, then the next she was in the water.'

'I've expressed my doubts about Lady Della to my brother already. When I tell him what we suspect, I do not believe he will consider her.'

'I doubt he will consider me either, a drowned rat looking as I am.'

'Of course he will. Especially when he sees how well you dance.'

With that he swept her up in a pose. He had been thinking of a dance lesson before all the mayhem broke out.

'I've never danced with a drowned rat,' he admitted. 'One, two, three.'

He spun her about the grass. He would like to say her skills had improved with his previous instruction, but could not. She stepped on his toes twice, almost toppled over once.

Of course, it had only been a day and she was attempting to dance in a wet gown. He still had two more days.

'It is such a shame that Lady Kirkwynd is leaving us so soon,' Aunt Adelia declared. 'If you can say nothing else about her, she is entertaining.'

Ginny had come down to breakfast early at Aunt Adelia's request. Now here she sat between the Dowager and her aunt, nibbling toast and getting an odd feeling that the three of them sharing such an early meal was not by chance.

Not that she minded getting up early—she preferred it, in fact. The fresh, sweet scents of morning, sunshine streaming over the fells along with the twitter of happy birds. It was the best time of day.

It had not escaped her notice that Will was also an early riser. She would not admit this to anyone, especially her breakfast companions, but she rose early enough each day to watch him while he went about his early morning business. From what she had learned, he began his day by spending a few moments on the dock, gazing out at the lake.

She wondered if he was giving thanks for being allowed to live on this beautiful estate.

It was what she would do if she lived here. Perhaps she would even join Will at the edge of the dock.

Of course, if she lived here it would be because she was Phillip Talton's wife and would begin her day with him.

For a moment she forgot to chew. The piece of toast she had been nibbling dropped out of her fingers and on to her plate.

Was this something she could even do? Wed one man while she woke each morning looking for his brother to walk past her chamber window?

Thought of in that way, she would be committing a great sin!

Clearly her feelings for William Talton were complicated. He was her friend…but could he be more? Did she even want him to be more, possibly risk changing what was already between them?

Their friendship was what she cherished. Deeply cherished. Would wedding Phillip change that friendship? Her heart would break if it did.

It only stood to reason that marriage would change something. Her loyalties would naturally shift from Will to her husband.

There was every chance she was worrying about it for no reason since it was unlikely that she would be Phillip's choice anyway.

After all, there were several ladies here who would make an excellent countess.

In all likelihood she would be going home next

week, an event which would also alter her friend-ship with Will.

The thought of going back to life as it was be-fore coming to Hawkwood made her feel quite blue.

Back then she had missed the memory of the boy she spent the day with. Now that she had come to know the man…well, she would be be-yond blue.

How interesting that it was not the idea of missing Phillip that first hit her. Although, she would. He was a likeable man…a fine man.

'I shall miss the drama which accompanied her.' The Dowager's thin lips twitched at the cor-ners. 'But when a letter calls one home…home one must go.'

'Indeed, one must. At least the house will be safe from the dog's relentless chewing.'

She could only wonder and wait to discover where they were guiding this conversation.

With a slow sip of warm chocolate, Ginny thought about the dog, decided she would miss him and his well-placed mischief.

'I find it rather sad that she feels she must leave.' Believing that the push might have been deliberate, Ginny did feel some sympathy for the woman.

'Oh, quite, I'm sure, but she was not well suited to my son, so it is for the best.'

'Yes, indeed! There are several young ladies in attendance worthy of his consideration,' her aunt said with a quick smile at Lady Hawkwood. A smile, yes…but somehow Aunt Adelia managed to convey a wink without even closing an eye. 'But, Ginny, you will be acquainted with them in a way we old ladies are not. Who do you feel is worthy of winning him?'

'You know my feelings, Auntie. Lady Talton, I do not believe this is a matter of being worthy… or of winning. It is about who your son sees a happy future with…someone he finds an emotional connection with. It is possible that the future Lady Hawkwood is not even in attendance.'

'But I have no doubt that she is.' Violet Talton slanted Ginny the oddest glance. There was some hidden meaning to it, but since the Dowager was skilled at hiding her thoughts, Ginny could not imagine what she meant by it. 'With so many lovely ladies cooing over him I have no doubt he shall be smitten with several of them.'

The Dowager turned a pursed-lipped smile on her aunt. 'Don't you agree, Adelia?'

'He could not fail to be smitten...but, Ginny, my dear, with whom is what we seek to discover.' Her aunt tapped her chin in thought. 'Perhaps you might know something...perhaps have heard talk.'

'I can honestly say I have not.'

'I think Lady Della might suit.' Surely the Dowager did not mean it. 'She is quite pretty and from a good family. I have seen my son look at her in a...a special way, shall we say?'

'Of all of them...' Ginny felt compelled to point out the truth '... I would pick her last.'

'My goodness, Ginny,' her aunt said with a smile and a lift of her brows. 'Do I hear a note of jealousy in your voice?'

'Yes, Adelia, I think you might. I hear it clearly enough. Well, Ginny dear, Phillip is a handsome man and if you were a tiny bit green it would be understandable. It might mean you have a special feeling for him.'

She was not a bit green. Why was that? If what they hinted at...all right, more than hinted at, was true, she ought to be.

Since she was not, this might be something to give a deal of thought to.

While she did not expect to be in love with the Earl when they wed, but had every hope that she would in time…then she ought to begrudge the other women's attention towards him.

Oddly, she did not feel green when maybe she ought to.

'It's only that I have reason to know she is not worthy of Phillip.'

'Oh…and why is that?' Aunt Adelia asked.

'She misplaces her hats…or so I have heard.'

'Oh, yes.' Her aunt arched a knowing brow. 'That is rather a disqualification.'

'Who, then?' Phillip's mother asked, with a glance at Aunt Adelia.

'Lady Elizabeth.' The answer came to her easily. 'I think they would be brilliant together.'

'She does seem a dependable sort, indeed,' Lady Hawkwood admitted. 'But is she…well, how do I put this?'

'Frolicsome?' Aunt Adelia suggested.

'I cannot say that I've heard her laugh.' The Dowager levelled a gaze at Ginny. 'You, my dear, have a lovely laugh.'

And there it was. The reason for this private

breakfast. They did not wish to know which lady she thought would suit Phillip. The matchmakers wanted to know if she thought she would suit him.

She had no answer, naturally. It was something she also wished to discover. If anything, this breakfast had raised more questions than answers.

What she did know was that she had expressed her 'lovely' laugh far more often with Will than with anyone she had ever known.

Still, if laughter was a qualification for marriage, she had never heard of it.

Given which, marriage to Phillip was not necessarily ruled out. A brilliant match might be made, founded upon deep affection, even if a couple did not spend humorous moments together.

One thing she did know, the questions raised over breakfast left her greatly confused.

'I wonder...' Ginny stood up from the table '...if laughter is the gauge of a good marriage, ought I find Lady Kirkwynd and plead with her to stay? You must admit, she does have an engaging laugh. Surely Lord Hawkwood will be captivated by it.'

Which was what Ginny was trying not to do while she rushed out of the dining room—laugh.

Oh, but it was difficult because both Aunt Adelia and Lady Hawkwood looked like nothing if not a pair of blinking owls, distressed that their prey had just escaped down a rabbit hole.

After breakfast, with some members of the party shooting arrows at targets, the rest were free to seek their own entertainment.

For couples it was a time to sneak away for a private walk along the lake.

For some of the ladies it was time to gather and chat. While she was getting better at joining in social conversation, it was still not her first choice for passing the time.

For Ginny, this meant time with her journal. She already knew what she would write about. Coming outside, she was reassured that it could be nothing but the pristine beauty of a summer morning in Ullswater.

How, she wondered while walking towards 'her' writing bench, would she bear the noise and the sooty air of London when she went home?

Writing about closed-in spaces, the calls of vendors selling their wares and the rumble of carriage traffic going past Cliverton's walls, would not be nearly as pleasant. But then, not all writing needed to be pleasant.

'Oh! Lady Ginny.' Lady Della rushed up to her. 'Have you heard the news?'

'It depends upon which news you are speaking of.'

'The best news, of course!' Lady Della clapped the tips of her fingers in clear delight. 'Lady Kirkwynd is taking her miserable little dog and going home.'

'Yes, I've heard it.' For a second, Lady Della appeared crestfallen to not have been the one to relay the gossip, but she rallied quickly.

'It is for the best if you ask me.' Lady Della lowered her voice. 'Here is something else. I've heard a rumour that tonight we will be playing... games.'

She whispered the last word, as if 'games' was somehow a naughty word.

'Games?'

Eyes wide and blinking, she revealed, 'Games with kissing forfeits.'

'Kissing forfeits?'

'Surely you've had to pay them? Really, Ginny, they are popular. It was your own aunt who arranged the game and the penalties, so how wicked could it really be?'

'My aunt does enjoy a spot of…of fun.' Indeed, Aunt Adelia would consider it an innocent pastime where everyone would laugh and be merry.

'The thing to remember is, do not let a man's shadow fall upon you—that is how one pays the penalty. If you do, you will be forced to forfeit a kiss.'

'How…dreadful?' William's smile flashed in her mind…not Phillip's. She would have given that more thought if Lady Della were not peering at her so intently…waiting for her reaction.

'It can be.' Lady Della giggled. 'Or not be. Who would you want to kiss you?'

'I shall simply do my best to avoid shadows,' she assured Lady Della…and herself, to be honest.

Really, she was too confused about her feelings to be kissing anyone.

She continued to walk towards her favourite bench.

'Are you going to write in your little book?' Lady Della asked, following at Ginny's elbow. 'About Justine?'

Drat it.

'The weather.'

Hurrying away from Lady Della, she sat down, took off her bonnet, then set it beside her on the bench. She opened her writing valise, took out her pen, then opened her journal. A gusty breeze ruffled the pages.

Drat it again. With only the word 'sunshine' scratched on the page, she felt the planks on the bench give.

'You seem quite devoted to writing about the weather. This is not the first time I've seen you at it.' Lady Della craned her neck, trying to see what Ginny had written. 'I would so love to read about that Admirable person's opinion of it.'

Ginny snapped the journal closed. The last thing she wanted was for anyone to read what was on these pages. They were for her eyes and no one else's!

'It must be something quite scandalous for you to— Oh, look, there she is.'

Glancing towards the porch, she spotted Lady Kirkwynd coming down the front steps wearing travelling clothes, small Bernard tucked into the crook of her arm.

Lady Della stood, giving a lingering glance at the journal. 'I am glad to see the last of her and that awful dog. It will be so much easier to win the Earl without her getting in the way.'

'We all want the same thing for the Earl, do we not? For him to find a good match? We are not in competition with each other, Lady Della.'

'Humph…even so, her departure is a boon for us all.'

Lady Della walked away, but not far. She stood on the grass, gazing out at the lake.

All at once, the wind caught Ginny's bonnet, picked it up and spun it away towards the water.

Hurriedly, Ginny dropped her pen and raced after it. It was such a delicate thing, the prettiest hat she had. She would be crushed to see it ruined.

Catching it in the last second before it rolled into the water, she breathed a sigh of relief, then turned back towards the bench.

Lady Della! Oh, the wretch! She had taken Ginny's moment of distraction to return to the bench and snatch up the journal. Her eager fingers were even now flipping through the pages.

Ginny would never make it back before Justina and Lord Handsome and Bold were exposed to her greedy eyes.

But wait! There was Lady Kirkwynd, sitting

down beside Lady Della. Looking like a woman with a score to be settled, she gave Lady Della a flat-lipped smile. She set Bernard on the lawn where he took a sudden interest in the hem of Lady Della's skirt.

When the Baroness flicked her hand to shoo him away, she knocked the journal from Lady Della's fingers. It fell on the grass beside the pup.

'How clumsy of me.' Lady Kirkwynd bent to pick it up, but slowly, giving Bernard enough time to snatch it.

He dashed madly across the lawn, gripping the journal in his sharp little teeth, his tail wagging merrily.

'You scamp!' Lady Kirkwynd leapt up from the bench, lifted her skirts and chased the pup across the grass.

Ginny pursued them both.

Lady Kirkwynd went down on her knees, whistled to Bernard. He turned about and scampered back to her. It took some coaxing and cooing, but she managed to pry the journal from him.

Standing, the Baroness handed the book to her. 'Honestly, a woman's journal is for no one's eyes but her own. I'm sorry about the teeth marks,

Lady Virginia. It was the only way I could think of to get it away from that snooping girl. Honestly, I hesitate to call her a woman. Debutantes can quite ruin a gathering, if you ask me.'

'You have my thanks.' She bent to pet the pup's head. 'Thank you, too, my little hero.'

'Perhaps he is, but the only thing he had in mind was chewing it up.'

'I'm sorry you feel you must leave, Lady Kirkwynd.'

'Truly? I think you are the only one, then.'

She could not think of how to reply since it was probably so.

'William will miss you, I think,' she pointed out.

'He might, at that.' She smiled, shrugging, then bent to pick up Bernard. 'But I am glad we have a few moments alone before I leave... I was meaning to speak to you about something.'

Ginny could not imagine what. They barely knew each other.

'You will know I have been married.'

'Yes, you are a widow I have been told.'

'A greedy manipulative one, no doubt. But the truth is I know what a happy marriage should be. Despite what people say, I did love my husband.

It never mattered to either of us that he was so much older than I was. But to the point of what I wanted to say…having made a love match, I know it when I see one. I have noticed how you are with Lady Hawkwood's son. It is my opinion, which you may take or leave, that you suit each other very well.'

'I like him well enough, but Lord Hawkwood and I—'

'I am referring to her second son, to William. Trust me, I have seen the way he looks at you… and the way you look at him.'

That moment, Lady Kirkwynd spotted her carriage driver waiting for her at the foot of the steps.

'Ah, I must be on my way.' She scooped up Bernard. 'It is none of my business,' she said. 'Please take my observation or discard it as you wish to.'

'I'm sorry you must leave.' And Ginny found that she actually was sorry.

'It has become clear to me that the Earl and I will not suit and I am needed at home.' With a nod, she turned and walked towards her carriage.

Well, my word…what was she to think of Lady Kirkwynd's revelation?

What was to say she was correct, other than that she had once had a happy marriage?

But a love match? She saw that between her and Will?

Take it or leave it, indeed. Having heard her observation, Ginny found it was difficult to dismiss.

Chapter Nine

'I beat you again.' Phillip grinned at him while they walked with the other archers back towards the house.

'Today, only,' William pointed out. 'Last time I beat you.'

'I'm improving. Next time I'll shave the feathers off your arrow.'

It was true, Phillip was improving, not only at archery but in his spirit, as well. Day by day he sensed his brother healing. He smiled more quickly than he used to. He laughed more freely.

William had to admit that his mother's idea to host this country party was an excellent one. Even if his brother did not find a bride among the ladies, he had at least reclaimed his joy in life.

'I need to begin spending time alone with a few of the ladies…not quite alone, of course. But perhaps you would come along. Four of us going out on some excursion would be appropriate.'

'After lunch?' William suggested. 'A boat ride around the lake would suit your purpose. Who would you choose?'

Phillip clapped him on the shoulder. 'Thank you, Brother. I would like to begin with Ginny and Elizabeth. They get along well so it should be a pleasant afternoon.'

Ginny was an excellent choice…he could not be more pleased. Spending an afternoon on the *Raven* with her would be delightful. He would enjoy it as much as Phillip would.

More than Phillip would…the thought was but a whisper in his mind, there and banished in a heartbeat.

'You knew Ginny from before. I wonder, is she the girl you remember her to be?'

Yes, and more.

'Everyone grows up. Naturally, she is different to how she was as a child…but in many ways she is much as I recall her to be.'

'You must have been pleased to see her again?'

Phillip was looking at him strangely. For the life of him, William could not decipher his expression.

'Nothing quite like being reunited with an old friend,' his brother added. If Phillip knew how to wink, William thought he would have, but he did arch a brow.

What was he really asking?

Since he could not begin to imagine, he answered the question asked out loud.

'I was very happy to see her, of course. Let's have lunch and then find out if she and Elizabeth wish to come out with us.'

Ginny stood beside Phillip on the deck of the *Raven*, watching while they sailed past green trees and greener pastureland.

Fresh air blew softly across her face, ruffling the hair at her temples and neck.

'I cannot think of a nicer way to spend the afternoon than this,' she said. 'Thank you for inviting me.'

'Nor can I, even though I have made the trip around the lake more times than I can count.'

'I imagine it changes with the weather and the season so it is never commonplace.'

'So true. It even changes with the time of day. Or it transforms according to the company one keeps.' He really did have an engaging smile. A woman could do worse than waking to it every morning. 'Spending time with you and Lady Elizabeth is just what this day needed. I'll admit that getting away for a while is refreshing.'

Phillip pointed to the lower deck where Will and Elizabeth leaned against the rail, chatting and laughing.

And why should they not be laughing? Will was a man who enjoyed company…he also enjoyed laughing. She should not be as foolish as to believe it was something he did with her alone.

It was just…well…he was pointing to a pair of ducks waddling on the shore and Ginny felt—

'My brother seems to enjoy Lady Elizabeth's company, don't you think?'

Phillip looked at her with an expression she could not quite understand. His brows arched, causing a crease between them. He was not smiling…not with his mouth, but she thought one lurked behind his eyes.

'He would, of course,' he added. 'She is very lovely. Come, let's go down and join them and see what has them in such fine humour.'

Ducks.

She gave herself a mental shake. It was foolish to begrudge him sharing the humour of them with Elizabeth.

Surely the Good Lord created such funny birds for everyone's amusement.

Will must have heard their steps crossing the deck because he turned, smiling.

As always, his dimples made her warm all over. Funny how a simple gesture could make one feel that life was bright and wonderful.

Did Will's smile make Elizabeth feel the same way?

Perhaps not. For all that she appeared to be having a delightful time with Will, Ginny could not fail to notice the way Elizabeth's gaze tended to linger on Phillip.

From the beginning Ginny had thought the two of them would suit. Of course, it did not matter what she thought, it was what Phillip thought that counted.

Coming to the rail, Phillip took a place between Will and Elizabeth, which put Ginny beside Will.

'Did you see them?' he asked.

'See who?'

'The mallards.' He pointed towards the shore.

'I was hoping you had. I wonder if they have a nest close by.'

'Elizabeth must have enjoyed seeing them.' She really should not be so relieved to know he had been thinking of her while laughing with her friend.

'I do not think she appreciated their unique nature. Her comment was that they were messy.'

Oh, well…good, then. 'There is that, but—'

'Let's walk.' He caught her hand, then tucked it into crook of his elbow.

'Is it rude to leave them alone?' she asked with a glance back over her shoulder.

'Ruder to hover nearby when Phillip has courting on his mind.'

'He plans to begin courting?' This was wonderful news. Good for Phillip!

'It is on his mind.' He was not looking at her while he spoke, but at the water rushing past the hull. 'Ginny, how would you feel about it if he decided to court you?'

Was she distressed by his question? Uncomfortable with him prying into her feelings?

Maybe, since she did not answer, but gazed

steadily at the shoreline while the boat chugged slowly along.

What had got into him, asking such a thing?

Perhaps it was because of their friendship that he felt he could probe her heart.

Or it might be because he needed to sort the intentions of the ladies competing for Phillip. Which made no sense when it came to Ginny since he well knew her intentions were sincere.

Looking up from the water, he watched her in profile...how sunlight glimmered in her fair hair, the way the breeze lifted loose strands, fluttered them back from her face.

'I'm sorry, I should not have asked. It is not my business.'

She looked at him then, her eyes a match to the clear blue sky. Her pretty pink lips pressed together in thought and he found he could not look away from them.

Blame it, but it was his business! If Ginny was to be his brother's wife...his attraction to her was completely inappropriate.

What he was to do about it he could not imagine. What he could imagine, and all too vividly, was kissing her.

'It is a fair question.' Her answer snapped him

out of the enchantment he had fallen into while staring at her mouth. 'Your brother had a loving marriage to Cora. You want that for him again so it is your business.'

He gave himself a good mental shake to clear what had to be the besotted expression melting his features. But to be fair, she was exceptionally beautiful so it was no wonder he should think of kissing her.

Being a healthy male, Will felt his reaction was natural, understandable…and certainly no betrayal of his brother. What he ought to be wondering about was—did Phillip feel the same draw towards Ginny as he did? Was there natural attraction between them which would give Phillip the sort of deep bond he had shared with Cora?

'You love your brother and do not wish to see him make the wrong choice.'

The urge to smooth the blowing strands behind her ear was nearly more than he could resist. He clamped his hands on the rail. 'Yes, that's a part of it. But I would not want to see you make the wrong choice either.'

She slid her hand across the rail. Her delicate,

fair-skinned little finger brushed his, covered it and squeezed.

His gaze jerked down, fastening on the spot where their fingers joined. No touch had ever felt so innocent, yet at the same time so intimate. He could not recall a simple gesture ever crashing into his heart the way this one did.

'Will, I promise to be careful. Phillip has suffered so much already. You can trust me not to do anything to hurt him.'

Nor would he. Nothing could make him betray his brother.

Ginny Penneyjons was his dear friend. No matter how confused his feelings towards her were, she would remain as such.

But, a sneaky voice in his mind suggested, what if Phillip did not choose her?

What if it was Elizabeth or one of the other ladies his brother developed a bond with?

'Do you suppose they are missing us yet?' he asked.

He did not want to re-join them, but clearly it would be for the best. Until Phillip made his choice, it might be wise to spend less time in Ginny's company.

'Elizabeth isn't.'

Hopefully Phillip wasn't missing them either. Because if he wasn't, it would mean…nothing.

Again, he must not allow his focus to wander from his brother's happiness.

After dinner Ginny tried to hide away in her chamber, feigning an ailment, but Aunt Adelia would not have it.

'This will be great fun!' Her aunt kept a firm grip on Ginny's elbow, all but towing her towards the parlour. 'You might even get a kiss from the Earl.'

'I've been told this kissing forfeit was your idea.'

'Indeed. Brilliant, was it not?'

'Not… Really, Auntie, why would you propose such an unseemly game? I can hardly credit that Lady Hawkwood would agree to it.'

'Don't be silly. It is a common game which no one takes as more than a spot of fun.'

'I disagree. This will be the most embarrassing evening of my life.'

'Not if you answer the three questions correctly.' Aunt Adelia's blue eyes winked in pure and delighted mischief.

'No one answers them correctly, as you well know.'

'Oh, but, Ginny, you have been doing so much better lately. No one would guess you used to be shy.'

'There is no used to be about it.'

'I've noticed you are relaxed in Phillip's company and, really, that is all that matters.'

'I will not be relaxed if I am required to kiss him in front of everyone.'

Aunt Adelia paused a few feet from the doorway to grin merrily and pat Ginny's cheek.

'I suppose you might make an arrangement with the Earl...perhaps meet him in private to pay the forfeit.'

'I will not go in there.' Ginny planted her slippers firmly on the highly polished floor.

For one, she did not wish to stand in the centre of the room, all eyes upon her while she answered three silly questions. And for two, she had no intention of being kissed in public or in private.

A man's heavy step clicked the floor behind her.

'Will you go in with me?'

Aunt Adelia's hand fell away and a firm, masculine one cupped her elbow.

'Hello, Will.' She placed her hand on his arm

because she would have drawn attention to herself had she struggled to escape this evening's nonsense. 'Please tell me you are not going to play my aunt's silly game.'

'I'm going to play it.' He grinned. 'And I am going to enjoy it.'

'There's the spirit!' Aunt Adelia declared, slipping her hand into the crook of Will's other elbow.

Seeing an empty place on the couch, Ginny sat down.

How many gentlemen's gazes had followed her across the room, now lingering upon her? She did not dare to look, but she felt them…oh, indeed, they were anticipating her owing forfeits.

She glanced up at Will where he stood beside the arm of the couch. She had not expected to see him frowning, but he glanced about the room, looking less than pleased.

He grunted, then bent down to whisper in her ear. 'I begin to see why you do not wish to play. Do not worry, though. I'll have a word with my brother and we will make sure it is only one of us your shadow falls upon.'

Straightening, he walked to the fireplace where his brother chatted with Lady Della and Jane.

At least that was something. If she had to play this game, it would be with two men she felt at ease with. Glancing about at the women in the room, she realised it was not only the gentlemen anticipating forfeits.

Naturally, all the young ladies, even the older ones, would wish to pay a forfeit to the handsome Earl. He was the prize to be taken at the end of the house party, after all.

Oh, but there in the corner was a young couple making eyes at each other. They would be paying penalties exclusively to one another.

Violet Hawkwood sat down beside Ginny.

'I've no doubt this will be amusing,' she said drily.

Yes, well, it would be if Ginny did not have to participate. To simply sit and see what came of the forfeits would be amusing.

With everyone gathered about, some seated and some standing, Aunt Adelia clapped her hands.

'Ginny, my dear!' Her aunt sounded as cheerful as a bird in springtime. 'We shall begin with you.'

'Just as well get it over with,' the Dowager

said, giving her elbow the slightest push up. 'I'm only glad I am too old to participate.'

The rules of the game were that she must leave the room while three questions were discussed which she would be required to answer either 'yes' or 'no' to.

Answering correctly and avoiding the forfeit would be easy except for the fact that she must answer without knowing what the questions were.

Standing on the far side of the closed door, she heard laughter. She rolled her eyes because, clearly, humour was going to be had at her expense.

No matter what, she would be embarrassed. She could do one of two things about it...three if she faked a faint. Even she was not that much of a jellyfish. She did have a backbone and she intended to use it. She chose to smile and not wither.

The door opened and Lady Della waved for her to come back into the room.

Everyone's attention was focused upon her. She reminded herself that there was nothing mean spirited intended in the game. Each of the ladies would face three questions this evening.

Calling upon a smile, she sought a friendly face so the gesture would appear sincere.

Glancing about, she did see two faces...no, three, which put her at ease. There was Will—as always, she would find assurance in his grin. But there was also Phillip and Elizabeth to focus her smile upon.

'Ginny,' Aunt Adelia announced. 'What is the answer to question one...yes or no?'

Borrowing her aunt's gesture of tapping her chin, she put on a pose of giving the matter a great deal of thought, even though either answer was sure to be wrong.

'Perhaps,' she stated with a firm nod.

Everyone chuckled.

Oh, well, then. She felt rather good all of a sudden.

'Sly girl,' her aunt declared. 'The answer must be yes or no.'

'No.'

Outright laughter swept the room.

'Oh, dear. The question was, "Do you find our host amusing?" Very clearly you owe a forfeit on that one. Now...what is your answer to question two?'

'Yes?'

'"Number of hours in a day?" was the question. Another forfeit, I fear.'

'But, Aunt Adelia, yes could be correct since there are hours in a day.'

Her aunt shook her head, her eyes a-glitter. 'The answer is not correct. Perhaps you will do better at question three.'

'I suppose I must answer "no".'

Whatever the question was, her answer made even the polished Dowager laugh out loud.

'Oh, brilliant!' Aunt Adelia clapped her hands. 'The question was, "Will you pay your forfeits?" No is a wrong answer.'

With a playful curtsy, Ginny took her place back on the couch while everyone applauded.

Now that the ordeal was over, she found it had not been so horrible—in fact, she had rather enjoyed it. Now that her turn was finished, she was free to relax and laugh with everyone else.

At least until the forfeits came.

The point of the game had come.

Forfeits…salutes…kisses.

It would be interesting to see to what degree the penalties were paid.

For William, it would be sweet and discreet

kisses to blushing cheeks or the backs of hands presented to him.

Casting a glance at his brother, he wondered what Phillip would do. Kissing hands was what he thought...unless one of the ladies was special to him.

Ginny was special to him, William already knew that. With some effort he managed to breathe past the sick feeling in his stomach the thought caused.

His mother signalled for the lamps to be turned down so that the only light in the room was cast by the fireplace.

She directed the gentlemen to stand along the opposite wall.

They took their places eagerly, shifting from foot to foot in anticipation of being the first to fall under the shadow of whichever lady must pay her forfeit.

Who would be first? The ladies hung back, some looking nervous and some coy.

The one stepping forward first sparkled. In William's mind Aunt Adelia had always been a flute of champagne with bubbles popping happily over the rim.

This evening was no different.

He stepped towards her, eager to show his long-time affection with a kiss on her cheek.

As it happened, he was not quick enough because Lord Helm rushed past him.

He kissed Adelia's hand.

'There's one forfeit paid,' he merrily announced.

When a smiling young man stepped forward the old man waved both William and the fellow off.

Everyone laughed when Lord Helm kissed the debtor on her blushing cheek.

'Forfeit two accounted for!' He rubbed his hands together, gleefully anticipating collecting the last one.

'I salute you, my lady,' he said and then placed a quick kiss on her lips.

Cheers rocked the room.

Aunt Adelia pressed her fingertips to her cheeks in mock embarrassment. She sat down on the couch next to his mother.

Mother shot her friend a reproving glance. What an odd pair they were. So different from one another and yet the very closest of friends.

'Virginia,' Mother called, her smile restored. 'Step forward and pay your penance.'

Ginny cast the line of men an uneasy glance.

At his mother's signal to 'go', they would fall over each other to claim a prize from the most beautiful woman they had likely ever laid eyes upon…at least in his opinion.

Ginny cast him an anxious glance.

He nodded at Phillip.

Together they rushed forward before Mother's signal.

Given this was a friendly gathering, even the bested gentlemen laughed at the Talton boys' eagerness.

For William, the eagerness was not feigned. All it took was to hear Ginny's relieved sigh and he was lost…wanting this kiss very badly.

Phillip nodded, indicating William should claim the first forfeit.

'Lady Virginia.' He had not meant to whisper, but where was his voice? 'I claim my prize.'

She smiled, presenting her cheek.

Petal soft with a scant scent of roses, her cheek was the sweetest spot he had ever placed his mouth. It must be why he lingered over it…why when she turned her face ever so slightly, he turned his.

No one watching would notice how the corners of their lips nearly touched. A sweet, if a bit longer than required, peck to the cheek was what they would see.

No one but Ginny heard him whisper her name in the instant he lifted his mouth. Not even she heard the groan in his soul when he gave his place to Phillip.

'I also claim a forfeit, my lady,' his brother announced with a grin.

Phillip also kissed Ginny's cheek, a quick buss accomplished in the space of a heartbeat. With a nod he stepped back, indicated that William should claim the last kiss.

Before he had recovered his wits from the first kiss, an eager fellow shoved between him and Phillip.

He picked up Ginny's hand and gave it an extremely heartfelt salute.

'You honour me, Lady Virginia,' he said and then took his place with the other gentlemen.

The man had been nothing but polite, respectful and admiring of Ginny.

Why then did William feel the urge to punch him?

'The evening was a great success,' Aunt Adelia declared while walking beside Ginny along the hallway leading to their chambers. 'I was so proud of you. If only your sisters could have seen you shine!'

'Or you, Auntie. Three kisses from Lord Helm?'

'Oh, but he is a dear old friend.' She waved her hand as if shooing away the observation…as if three kisses were nothing of note.

When they reached the chamber door, Aunt Adelia clasped Ginny's hands and squeezed them. 'And you got a kiss from Lord Hawkwood!'

'I am sure it did not mean anything. My hand was nearly devoured by Lord Smythe and I also paid a forfeit to Will.'

'William? Indeed, I noticed he was rather… cordial, shall we say?'

Ginny opened her chamber door. 'Oh, but he is a dear old friend.'

She shut the door, trying not to laugh at the expression on her aunt's face, but truly, she appeared stunned to have her words turned back on her.

Sitting down at her dressing table, Ginny plucked the pins from her hair, then put on her nightgown. Some of the guests required one of Hawkwood's maids for the service, but Ginny would not ask an overworked girl to do what she could do on her own. As it was, she was grateful that someone had lit a bedside lamp and left fresh water and towels.

Lying down on the bed, she pulled a soft quilt to her chin, then turned down the lamp.

She blinked at the ceiling.

Two kisses…all right, three, but the last from Lord Smythe did not signify. Everyone knew the fellow was mad for Lady Mary and had probably done it to make her envious.

But the other kisses, they did count…were greatly significant.

What she had learned from them was something she needed to give thought to.

The kiss that ought to have lingered on her cheek, the one that might hint at where her future lay, was quickly given…and quickly forgotten. It did not linger dreamily in her memory.

Oh, but the other. Even hours later, the memory of Will's kiss warmed her cheek. The more she thought about it, the warmer it got because had either of them turned their faces the tiniest bit…everything between them would have changed.

But had things changed between them anyway? Even without a real kiss?

It had been there, imagined between them. The way he whispered her name? It might as well have been a kiss.

Then again, perhaps she was reading a bit much into it. Even if there had been the thought of a kiss, Will had kissed all the ladies tonight, the older ladies on the cheeks and the younger ones on the hand.

And, yes, she had been paying attention to it. She ought not to assume her cheek was more special than any of the others. No, indeed. William enjoyed women's company. Everyone knew it.

A sudden gust of wind rattled the window, blowing it open. Throwing off the quilt, which had become rather suffocating anyway, she hurried to close it.

Looking out, she watched tree branches shift gently in the breeze, heard the leaves whispering. There were no clouds, only the bright full moon shining on the lake and the land. It was not likely that a storm was coming. That was good.

But something was coming…or someone, rather.

A dark figure strode across the lawn, walking on to the dock. Even as a shadow she knew him. When had she memorised the way he moved? When she was twelve…but he did move differently now than he had as a gangly adolescent.

She felt like dragging a chair to the window. How nice it would be to sit here and watch him. It would also be nosy. No one admired a voyeur. There was an alternative to watching out the window. She could get dressed and then go down to join him on the dock.

No, that would not do. Will did enjoy quiet moments and might not welcome an intrusion. An improper one at that.

The last thing a respectable lady ought to do was sneak out to meet a man in the middle of the night.

But was it not the purpose of the country party? For couples to get to know one another unencumbered by the strict social rules that prevailed in London?

If she went down—

Oh, just there…another shadow crossed the lawn. She was not certain, but she thought it was Phillip.

The figure joined Will on the dock. They

stripped off their outer garments. Squeezing her eyes shut, she felt for the window, then closed it. In the second before she secured the latch, she heard a pair of splashes. The brothers loved each other. She knew from having sisters how tight the bond could be.

Getting back in bed, she tugged the covers back under her chin, staring once again at the ceiling.

This time she was not thinking of how pleasant a kiss could be, but how destructive. What if she happened to kiss Will for real...discover that she was in love with him? What if, at the same time, Phillip decided to pick her as his wife? The very last thing she was going to do was come between brothers.

There was but one thing to be done.

Under no circumstances, be it a game or, well, whatever the circumstance, would she kiss anyone.

William surfaced, shaking the water from his face and nose.

He glanced up at Ginny's window. She had been standing there a moment before he went into the water, her figure cast in moonlight and her hair ruffled by the wind.

He'd nearly turned to wave for her to come down and join him. It seemed a natural thing to do.

By some stroke of luck, Phillip had come out to join him in a late-night swim. It would have been folly to be alone with her. Especially since he had come within a hair of kissing her fully on the lips. Had it not been for Lord Smythe's intervention, who knew what might have happened?

He dared not think of how he might have done something to ruin his brother's chances of finding happiness with Ginny.

While he could not be certain it was Ginny his brother liked best, he could not discount it either.

If it was William making a choice…but it was not. He would not consider marriage until his brother was happily settled. And probably not after that.

Phillip broke the water a few feet away, whooped and shook out his hair. 'It's brisk!' he sputtered through the water sluicing down his face.

'You needed to cool off after all the kissing you did tonight.'

'It was an entertaining evening. Remind me to thank Aunt Adelia. But you must admit, as pleasurable as the game was, it did not inspire a fellow to become hot and bothered,' Phillip said.

William would admit it—except perhaps he had.

'I have invited Lady Della and Jane for a visit to the waterfall tomorrow morning. May I count on you to help me get through it?'

'I thought you had discounted them.' Treading water, he shook water off his face.

'I think I do, but I'm still sorting things out. It would not be fair of me to make a choice until I have spent time with each one. Please say you will come.'

'I'll come.'

He could not help but wonder if his brother had made up his mind already, but felt duty bound to be honourable and not leave any of the ladies feeling she had not had a fair chance to present herself.

Phillip was always fair in his dealings.

William performed a neat flip, went back under the cold water trying not to think that his brother might already have chosen…that he might have chosen Ginny.

But once he wondered it, he felt the worst of brothers for hoping it was not true.

Perhaps he ought to remain down here with water over his head until all this was finished and his brother happily wed. Since he had no wish to drown, he stroked to the surface, renewing his resolve to be loyal to Phillip no matter what.

Chapter Ten

The writing desk of Adelia Monroe's bedchamber

My dearest and oldest friend Violet,
Please forgive the late hour of this communication, but something dire may have occurred. I could be wrong, but I fear that your younger son is developing a fondness for Ginny.
Whatever shall we do?

The writing desk in the bedchamber of Violet Talton—fifteen minutes later

My dearest and quite oldest friend Adelia,
You must have noticed that every man here has developed a fondness for your niece. Perhaps you are reading a bit much into it.
It is my boy's nature to be friendly. It is

why I gave him the job of keeping the ladies entertained. I'm sure this is nothing to be concerned about. My second son is loyal to a fault. No one is more dedicated to seeing Phillip happy than William is.

But I do have a concern. Have you noticed the way Elizabeth seems to have set her cap quite strongly for Phillip? While I like her quite well, a union between her and Phillip will not unite our families.

Sleep well, my dear, and do not to worry. All will work out for the best.

'William!'

Coming out of the stable, he turned at the sound of his mother's call. She walked towards him on the stone path beside the paddock.

One of the horses leaned over the rail and flapped its lips at her.

'Shoo,' she told it with a frown he knew to be false. Mother liked horses and the animals knew it.

'What are you doing out so early?' he asked, coming to meet her, then kissing her cheek. 'It's barely seven.'

'Looking for you.' She patted his cheek, giving him a smile which creased the corners of her eyes and lined her cheeks. He was reminded that she was no longer a young woman and it disturbed him.

But, in truth, many men his age were not as lucky as he was. To have one's mother reach a mature age was something many would envy.

Ginny would. What a blessing it was that she had her Aunt Adelia.

'We are hosting a ball tomorrow in case you have forgotten. I have been up since before dawn. With neighbours coming to join our guests, we will have nearly a hundred people here tomorrow.'

Forgotten? He could not have had he tried. Everything for the past several weeks had been leading up to the event. It had been every hand on deck, staff and sons alike preparing for it.

'You have hosted larger balls than this one.'

'But none of them with stakes this high. Even though the ball will be casual by society's standards, everything must be utterly romantic.'

'Since you are seeking me at this hour, I assume there is something I might do to help set the stage for romance?'

'Indeed. The florist made his delivery this

morning and I fear there are not nearly enough flowers. Nor enough candles. Since I cannot spare one of the servants to go about Ullswater and purchase them, I need you to do it.'

'Flowers and candles?' He gave his mother a slight bow, his hand over his heart. 'You may count on me for it.'

'You may take Lady Elizabeth along to help.'

That was an odd request.

'Why Lady Elizabeth?'

'Surely you have noticed she is demanding a great deal of your brother's attention.'

He had and did not think Phillip objected.

'Is there something about the lady you do not approve of? I will say, Mother, I do not find her objectionable.'

'Nor do I. It's only that she is not allowing Ginny enough time to get to know your brother.'

'Ginny? Not the others?'

'Indeed. She is such a lovely young lady and I think your brother is partial to her.'

In William's opinion he would be a fool if he were not. One thing Phillip had never been was a fool.

Perhaps Mother was correct that he should ask Elizabeth…only not for the reason she believed.

It had more to do with William spending less time with Ginny rather than Phillip spending more.

The more time he spent with her… Well, he just should not, that's all.

'I will ask Elizabeth if you think it will help. I just wonder, though.' He gave his mother a stern look that he knew she would not take seriously. 'Is Ginny your choice? Will you promote her to him even if he is drawn to another lady?'

'I know a woman's heart, my dear young dart-about. If you were to settle your attention on one lady long enough, you might, too. But Phillip will be happiest with Ginny. You may trust me on it.'

She was correct about William not spending enough time with any one woman to see deeply into her heart.

All except the one his mother clearly had in mind for his brother.

Years ago, he and Ginny had looked into each other's hearts. Seen the sorrow in one another's souls, cheered each other with laughter and high spirits. It had been so easy and innocent back then.

It was all different now. His feelings were changing. What began in friendship might be morphing into something else.

Something he could not allow.

Quite beyond his control his feelings towards her might become inappropriate. Only imagining Ginny and Phillip together, happy in their marriage and him standing by, watching covetously, made him feel the worst of cads.

If it came to it, he would go back to the sea… find work aboard a ship and never return home.

'Bring the carriage around after breakfast. Lady Elizabeth will come out to join you.'

'I have yet to ask her. And what about a chaperon?'

'No need to ask her, I did it this morning. As for a chaperon? In my opinion they are for London sensibilities. Since this is my house party, we shall continue to carry on without them. Besides, I trust you completely.'

'You know you can…and Elizabeth must be an early riser if you already asked her.'

She patted his cheek, then walked away. She cast a glance back over her shoulder. 'Enjoy your day with Lady Elizabeth.'

William brought his favourite carriage around at quarter of ten. This one was small, easy to manoeuvre and open to fresh air.

Lady Elizabeth was not waiting so he crossed

his arms over his chest, leaning back to watch the *Raven* glide past. The pleasant buzz of mid-morning activity swirling about made him smile.

What, he wondered, did his mother have planned for Ginny and Phillip while he took Elizabeth away for a few hours?

He made himself stop after a few seconds because he did not really want to know.

It was good that he would be spending the day with Elizabeth…safe. They got on well and he would not feel as though he had to fight temptation all morning long.

'Good morning, Will.'

He sat up with a start. 'Ginny!'

'I'm sorry. I know you were expecting Elizabeth, but she came down with a dreadful headache and asked me to come in her place.'

'I'd be lying if I said I was sorry.' Despite his recent thoughts, he did not regret it was Ginny he was helping into the carriage. 'Not that she has a headache, I don't mean that. But I'm not sorry to be spending the day with you.'

How could he be sorry? He enjoyed her company more than anyone's. But he did need to remain cautious…keep it uppermost in his mind that this woman was not intended for him but for his brother.

'Do you think your mother really needs more flowers?' Ginny asked while he climbed into the carriage and settled beside her. 'The lobby and the parlour already look like a florist's shop. If there is still a flower for sale within ten miles, I would be surprised.'

'We'll buy candles, then.' The carriage rolled along the drive. This was going to be a nicer day than he had expected…but again, he must not let his mind wander where it had no business wandering.

'Where are we going?'

'Penrith, first. Then on to Pooley Bridge. We can make a stop at Glenridding if we haven't found what we need.' He winked just to see her smile. 'If we are gone long enough, I might avoid being drafted into Mother's army. She is assigning tasks to everyone who appears to have an idle hand.'

Keeping Elizabeth away for the morning had been one of her tasks, but that situation had turned around nicely.

Spending time with Ginny was as far from a task as he could imagine. He did not want to know what Mother would have to say when she discovered his change of company.

'We could have lunch,' she suggested. 'That might take a while.'

'A nice leisurely lunch... I can eat slower than anyone you ever met when I put my mind to it.' The estate house fell from view as they travelled the lakeside road. 'We could be gone for hours. As long as I am not taking you away from something else you had planned?'

'Not anything I would rather do than this.' She plucked off her hat. Mid-morning sunshine touched her face for a moment before the carriage rolled into a grove of shady trees. 'Aunt Adelia mentioned something about an outing with Phillip, but Elizabeth spoke to me about her headache before your brother did and so here I am.'

It was as he suspected, then. The matchmakers had plans of their own regardless of what Ginny, Phillip or Elizabeth felt about it.

'Mother is going to be put out.'

'What do you mean? Why would she be?'

'You noticed my mother did not need flowers, probably not candles either. This excursion was to keep Elizabeth away from my brother.'

'Surely not! But why?'

'Because you were the one intended to spend

the morning with him.' A hank of fair hair blew across her lips. He should not, but he brushed it back behind her ear, felt the warm, soft curve of her cheek slide briefly under his fingers. 'Have you noticed that my mother and your aunt are matchmaking?'

She laughed, the sound hitting his heart like an arrow to a bullseye.

'They are not terribly subtle about it. I know it is farfetched to suggest, but honestly, Will, sometimes I wonder if this whole affair might have been designed to patch Phillip and I together.'

'I would not put it past them, but I, for one, am glad if they did. For whatever reason this house party came about, it brought you back to me… my long-lost friend,' he added quickly because what he said was far too telling.

'I'm glad, too.'

'Will it work, do you think?' He arched a brow to make light of the question he desperately wanted to know the answer to. He had asked it before, but still… 'Do you like my brother?'

'I have never made it a secret that I think he is a wonderful man. Your mother should be vastly proud of you both.' Coming out of the shade of overhanging trees, sunshine bore down hotter than it normally did. She put her hat back on and tied the ribbons under her chin. 'I think it is a blessed woman who has children who are as devoted as you and your brother are to each other. It isn't always so with brothers.'

She was correct, he was devoted. The proof of it lay in the fact that he did not pull the team over to the side of the road and kiss Ginny Penneyjons.

No matter what, he was not going to do that.

Blame it! He could not very well control where his imagination took him, but he could control what he did about it.

Kissing her that one time, which was not even a true kiss, but an accident...and the kiss to her cheek to pay a forfeit, those times were enough to warn him to be cautious when it came to Ginny.

'Would you be happy, though, living here at Hawkwood? It is nothing like London.' He watched her expression to judge if her eyes said something her lips did not. 'I know ladies who do not enjoy quiet country life.'

'I am not among them.' She smiled with her eyes as much as her pretty lips...the ones he was not going to consider kissing. 'Ullswater is exceptional. So beautiful and peaceful…and the truth is, with my sisters married there is nothing for me in London. You know me well enough, I think, to tell that I am not comfortable in society.'

'You would be dealing with it, though, if you married Phillip. Being Countess does involve a great deal of socialising, both here and in London.'

'At least I would not be sought after by…well, I would be married and it would make a difference.'

It hit him hard, hearing those words…harder than he wanted it to. Because, yes, she would be married…to his brother and it would make a difference.

A difference that made his soul feel as though it was being cut down the middle.

He would fight to keep the cost of his loyalty from showing. He had to! For the sake of everyone, he must not reveal his heart, not by glance or by word.

'Is it supposed to be this hot?' Ginny asked, leaning over a sturdy rail and gazing into the pool at the base of Aira Force. 'Do you think the candles will melt?'

Oh, but the mist from the fall was so lovely brushing her face. She took a slow, deep breath. Everything smelled fresh and green.

'This kind of heat is not typical.' Will stood beside her, also gazing down. She wondered if he were wishing for night to come so he could take his nightly swim in the lake. 'No need to rush back for the candles' sake. If they were going to melt, they would have done it by now. Besides, Mother didn't really need them.'

'I wish my toes were in the water.' The pool was as clear as a looking glass. The stones at the bottom appeared shimmery cold and inviting. 'No... I wish all of me was in the water.'

'If you marry my brother, you can swim in the lake whenever you wish.'

As nice as that sounded, it was not exactly an inducement for making a lifetime commitment.

'What else might I do?' she asked playfully, deciding to keep the light-hearted spirit of his comment.

'Take a ride on the *Raven* whenever you want to.'

'It is a nice boat ride. But to marry for it? I would need something more.'

'Hike the fells?'

'Not if it is this hot.'

'It hardly ever is.' Looking sharply up from the water, he shot her the grin that always made her want to laugh. 'You would get to have me as your brother.'

'Oh, well... I did always wish for a brother. I think you would make an excellent one.' Except that there was a small voice in her heart sounding a warning that it would be very wrong.

Apparently, he did not think it would because he sounded as if he would be pleased to have that family tie with her.

If warning bells were clanging in his mind, he hid them behind a friendly...and, yes, brotherly smile.

'Think about it, if you lived here, the three of us...you, me and Phillip could spend more days like this one.'

'It was a good day, wasn't it?'

'What did you like best about it?'

Spending time with him...the things they did were not what made it fun...just that they did them together.

'All right, then...if you really want to know?'

'If you tell me yours, I'll tell you mine.'

'It was when we stopped at Pooley Bridge for

lunch, then took a walk beside the water. Of course, I do not need to tell you what happened, but I shall because I want to commit it to memory.'

'It is burned into mine...right where I store all my shameful recollections. Being attacked by a swan is not something I want to recall.'

'Nevertheless, you did ask.' She took another deep breath of misty air, grateful for the respite from the heat. 'And you were my hero, stepping between me and the aggressive fowl. I made it to the top of the bank just in time to see the lovely creature hanging on to the seat of your trousers...squawking...flapping its wings as if it were mad as a hatter.'

'I'm not sure I have ever heard you laugh so hard,' he grumbled.

'True, my ribs are sore, but I can only wonder...' She leaned back, glancing behind at the beak-sized rip in his trousers.

'Sore.' He nodded, rubbed his posterior and grunted.

'Your turn,' she said. 'What was your favourite part of the day?'

'When I opened my eyes and found it was you

and not Elizabeth I was going to spend the day with.'

'Oh.' He did not say this in jest. She took his words into her heart, felt a flutter tickle her belly. 'But I'm certain you would have had a wonderful day with Elizabeth.'

'No, Ginny, I would not have.'

His dimples were not flashing while he gazed at her. Which was not to say there was not something flashing. He gave her a glance so compelling she had to look away.

It revealed an emotion she thought he might not wish to have revealed.

'I imagine they will be wondering where we are.' She pushed away from the rail.

'The team will be wanting their stalls,' he answered.

A stone stairway led back up to where the team was tethered in the shade.

Will caught her hand, held it. Both of them knew she was capable of making it up unassisted, yet neither of them let go of the other.

For all that she told herself it was a friendly gesture, she knew the delicious heat flashing between their palms did not have to do with the unusually hot weather.

Reaching the carriage, he did not help her up right away, but stood for a moment, looking into her eyes.

What did he see in them? she wondered. The same thing she saw in his?

Questions…uncertainty? What did the half-queasy turn of her belly mean?

She thought, perhaps, he felt more than common friendship for her…but he had also admitted that he did not wish to marry. She thought she felt more than that for him, too, but she had come here seeking marriage.

No wonder her thoughts were in turmoil.

As they turned out on the road towards Hawkwood, the sun beat down again, the cool respite of the falls a sweet memory.

'I wonder what Phillip and Elizabeth did today?' she asked, attempting to turn her mind elsewhere.

'Whatever it was, you can count on Mother not being pleased about it.' His gaze focused on the road ahead. 'My mother is determined to have you, Ginny.'

'I imagine Phillip will have something to say about it.'

'She usually gets what she wants. And honestly, my brother would be a lucky man to have you.'

And also, honestly, Ginny would be lucky to have a man like the Earl.

Unless…well, unless she had feelings for— But of course there was no 'unless'. She knew Will's desire not to marry.

At the end of it, all her misgivings might be for nothing. There were a few fine ladies wishing to wed Phillip.

Despite what his mother and her aunt might want, he might choose someone else.

Elizabeth was head over heels for Phillip. Who was Ginny to say he would not find a stronger connection with her friend?

There was William…he did not seem to think so. But for all he thought Phillip would choose her, he was not privy to every secret of his brother's heart.

And Ginny, she was not privy to the secrets of anyone's heart. She did not even fully understand the secrets of her own.

Only moments after dinner Ginny discovered just how correct she and Will had been to suspect she had already been selected to be Phillip's bride.

'My friends,' Lady Hawkwood announced when the gentlemen would have retired to the library and the ladies to the parlour. 'Given that it is still unusually warm, I propose we change the usual arrangement and walk beside the lake.'

'Yes,' Aunt Adelia added. 'We shall split up into pairs to make the walk more pleasant.'

Gentlemen glanced at ladies, ladies smiled at gentlemen deciding who they wished to spend time with.

'We have already arranged you into pairs,' the Dowager announced. 'Lady Monroe and I have written them down.'

Will's mother shuffled through the small notes she held.

'William, you will walk with Lady Della,' she announced.

To his credit, Will managed to maintain his smile.

'Phillip, my dear, your lucky partner is Ginny.'

No surprise, there. But truly, she was lucky. Spending time with the Earl was always agreeable and it was what she needed to do in order to understand where her heart was leading.

Her glance over at Will and Lady Della was brief and unsettling.

She shifted her attention back to Phillip.

His smile made her feel better, her emotions more grounded.

'My lady?' Phillip extended his elbow. 'May I have the pleasure of a stroll in the moonlight?'

While they walked away from the others, she noted how strong Phillip's arm was…how dependable it felt.

Any woman marrying this man would always feel secure. She had no doubt he would be a kind and respectful husband.

The question in her mind was…to whom?

'How was your day out and about with my brother?'

'Being with William is always entertaining. I quite enjoyed it.' What she wanted to know was how Phillip got on with Elizabeth, if indeed he managed to spend time with her. Between her 'headache' and the matchmakers' machinations, she had to wonder. 'And how was your day?'

'Quite nice, even though Mother kept me busy with things to be done for tomorrow night.'

'It was supposed to be Elizabeth going with William, but she came down with a headache.'

'She did mention it while we were directing the servants on where to place flowers in the ballroom. As luck would have it, she felt completely recovered within moments of you and William leaving.'

'How fortunate,' she said, which made him arch one brow at her and laugh.

It was a nice laugh. Looking at him in the moonlight, she thought his smile was also nice… comfortable.

'Mother did not think so, nor did your aunt.' He patted her fingers where they rested lightly in the crook of his elbow. 'If you want to know the truth, Ginny, I suspect they are trying to influence my choice.'

'Will and I were saying the same thing earlier today. Subtlety is not their strong suit, I'm afraid. I hope you are not offended at the way they are pushing us at each other. Aunt Adelia means well, I'm sure.'

'How could I possibly be offended that your aunt thinks I am worthy of you?' He stopped, stooped to pick up a stone, then gave it a toss, skipping it across the lake.

'That was very well done!' She was impressed— four full skips before the stone sank.

'I taught William how to do it when we were younger. He never got past two skips, though.'

'Are the pair of you always so competitive?'

'Not always. In the things that really matter we are not.' He nodded, smiling his easy smile. 'We have worked out the running of Hawkwood rather well...who is responsible for doing what. Practically speaking we both bear the title. It really is more of a job than one man can accomplish on his own. He does not try to advise me on Parliamentary business and I do not try to direct the operation of the estate.'

'I hope...' and she truly did hope this '...that if you choose a lady among us, she will not...' How did she say this and have it come out right? She half wished she had not begun the thought.

He must have known what was on her mind because he said, 'She will not come between me and my brother, do you mean?'

'Because it does happen, you know.'

'It did not for me and Cora. If anything, she promoted my relationship with William...the two of them got along quite well so there was never the tension of having torn loyalties.'

Torn loyalties were a wicked thing for a family to bear. One would live every day on edge. The very last thing she intended to do was cause such a rift.

But perhaps he would not choose her and she would go home, where her confused feelings for Will would not matter.

'I think Cora was a lucky woman.'

'It is flattering that you think so. She always told me I was the lucky one.'

'Well, I think that you both were.'

'I wonder,' he said softly, almost as if he were speaking to himself, but then he looked at her. 'Will I be lucky again?'

She was spared from having to answer by a bell being rung from the front porch.

'Ah… Mother's signal for everyone to return.'

Walking towards the house, they were joined by other couples, laughing and chatting.

William fell into step beside her, Lady Della on his arm. From the sound of her voice it seemed she was gossiping about someone.

Will glanced over at her, rolling his eyes.

Before they went up the porch steps, Phillip pressed her elbow, stopping her.

'I want to say, referring back to what we were

speaking of, if you were to marry into the family, I am confident you would not come between me and my brother. Just in case it was a concern to you, it need not be.'

With that, he escorted her up the stairs and into the house.

Was he suggesting he had made his choice? That he had picked her? But, no…that was not what he had said, exactly. Only that he thought she would fit into the family.

With a tiny pinprick to her heart, she wondered if it was true.

Once inside Lady Della and a couple of others rushed for the Earl, all of them nattering on at the same time.

'Did you enjoy your walk?'

Will smelled good. She recognised his outdoorsy, masculine presence beside her even before he spoke.

Glancing up, she noted the mischief in his grin.

'Of course. Far better than you enjoyed yours, I imagine.'

'Did you know that Lady Mary stuffs her bosom with stockings? That Lady Edna sings off key and Lady Myra's breath is not fresh?'

'No, but I did learn that when you skip stones you have never achieved more than two bounces.'

'Says Phillip…but come out to the dock later. I'll prove him wrong.'

Chapter Eleven

It was late.

Which was only the first reason she ought to ignore Will's invitation to watch him skip stones. Not to mention, she had already put on her night-clothes.

She wriggled her bare toes on the rug, deciding it was far wiser to remain in her chamber. Wiser and far safer.

Spending time alone with Will was beginning to make her feel off kilter...rather as if she were a big, soft, longing sigh pacing about her room on two uncertain legs.

What an odd image!

No respectable woman would consider going down there in the dark, her good judgement influenced by moonlight and magical starlight. Clearly fate was against her resisting temptation because, first…it was hot, which meant she had been forced to leave her chamber window open.

And then, clearly, she would not get cool air on her skin until she walked closer to it. Naturally, the closer she was, the more likely it was that she would look down.

Will might be there…on the dock. He might be stripping off his clothes for a swim. She might have been able to ignore the draw of cool air. Ignoring her natural curiosity was another matter altogether. So here she was, carried by no longer uncertain legs to the window.

As she suspected, he was out there, standing on the dock. But unlike in her imagination he was clothed…except, she thought his feet might be bare.

A small stack of stones lay on the deck within his reach. He stooped, picked one up, then gave it a toss without standing. One skip…two skips… sink.

She imagined she heard him grumble, but the shoreline was too far off to know for sure. Unable not to, she laughed.

Will pivoted slowly on the balls of his feet as if he had heard her. Oh…his feet were bare.

He glanced up at her with a grin, waving at her to come down.

According to societal rules, it would be vastly improper. The very last thing a girl ought to do. But she was not a girl, not in the same way as one newly debuted in society. Rather, she was a woman possibly making a decision about marriage.

She had questions. What made for a good marriage? Love and respect, clearly that. She did respect Phillip, admired him greatly and enjoyed his company.

Wasn't that all Mother felt for Father when she wed him? It was what she had told them. But she also loved to tell how, hours into their wedding night, she became completely besotted with Papa and by morning she was deeply in love.

But was she not already besotted with Will? He certainly made her heart beat hard and her stomach flutter. When she was with him…

Well, perhaps only Will held the answer to the question which mattered most. What did he feel for her? Friendship, yes, but was there more to it? If there was more, she needed to understand what it was. How could she even contemplate marrying Phillip until she did?

When Mama fell in love with Papa after only one night, there had not been Papa's charming brother to confuse her. Not only that, Papa was a man who'd wished to marry while Will claimed he did not wish to.

While society's rules did have their use, they did not for her...not tonight.

Being as late as it was, she doubted anyone was gazing out their window, anyway. Again, he waved for her to come down, a wicked and dimpled smile stretching his lips. Spinning about, she raced across her chamber, snatching her robe from the bed on the way. She did not take the time for slippers.

Will was barefoot so she would be, too.

It was a good choice to leave them behind. Her toes felt happy and free while she dashed across the grass. She heard no gasps of dismay coming from the windows above her. Glancing over her shoulder, she was relieved to see that no lamps were glowing.

She joined Will on the dock where he stood tossing a stone in the air and catching it.

'Your brother can make four skips,' she said.

'In his dreams.'

'No, I saw him do it only hours ago.'

'It was no doubt a trick of moonlight that made two skips look like four.'

'Ha! I heard four splashes. No trick of moonlight, Will.'

'Show me his technique.'

He glanced at the windows, just as she had, probably assuring himself that they were not being watched and their reputations would survive.

The thing of it was, she knew she was safe with him. A hundred chaperons would not make her any safer.

'I'd hate to give away his secrets.' She hugged her robe tighter about her because, feeling safe or not, she had never been in the presence of a man wearing her nightclothes.

Oh, but the night air did feel so fresh on her skin without heavy undergarments to keep it from whispering up her legs, over her hips and tummy.

'I already know his secrets.'

'And yet I saw you only make two skips,' she pointed out. 'But perhaps you will manage to once I show you how he did it.'

Her eyes slipped from his confident grin to the place where his shirt gaped open. He had smooth skin, slightly darker than most gentlemen's due to the time he spent out of doors. It gave him a decidedly masculine appearance which greatly appealed to her.

It was fascinating to see the muscles in his throat constrict and then relax, as if he was about to say something, but then did not.

Did it matter that she did not feel the same flutter for Phillip? Would it be something that came to her after the vows, the way it had for Mama?

'Show me,' he said.

Now she was good and stuck. She really had not paid attention to the way Phillip tossed stones.

With a wink he bent to pick up a flat oval-shaped rock. It felt cool and smooth when he placed it in her hand.

She stroked her fingers over it, then tossed it at Lake Ullswater. The stone sank without a splash.

'How odd,' she muttered. 'I was certain—'

He put another rock in her hand. This time he cupped his hand around hers and stood quite close.

'Let it rest in your palm, just so.' His instructions tickled her ear. 'Put your thumb here…your finger there.'

'All right, I've got it.'

And he had her. His fingers skimmed her wrist, leisurely up her arm to her elbow. He tugged down then sideways.

'The trick is to give it a good sidelong throw… spinning it some when you let go.'

Spinning when you let go? Well, she was doing that, clearly…only it hadn't to do with throwing the rock.

The stone plunked on water, again sinking without a skip. Except to the one it gave her heart.

How could she be standing here breathing when Will was so close…when she felt as though she was wrapped up by him? Hadn't the air been cool? Oddly, it felt as though she was breathing steam. She could hardly fill her lungs.

'Ginny, you seemed flushed.'

She nodded because her mouth had gone far too dry to utter words. Not that she could think of any to utter.

'Do you know how to swim?'

'Yes.' Oh, good, she could utter a word after all…but perhaps not the best one in the moment.

Before she could blink, he swooped her up in his arms. Giving a muffled whoop, he leapt off the end of the dock.

If he had been thinking, he would not have done it.

But he hadn't been thinking. Having landed in a situation where he was about to lose control and do the unthinkable, he carried them both into the water.

In his imagination he heard the water sizzle when they went under. It was a sizzle which had to be put out, ruthlessly drowned.

Now here he was, treading water face to face with the most endearing, dripping wet woman he had ever seen.

'Cooler?' he asked.

'Wetter, at least.' She blinked waterdrops from her lashes. She stroked backwards a few strokes. 'That is an extreme way to get out of trying to hide your inferiority at skimming stones.'

'Sometimes a man has no choice but to jump off the deep end.'

'Apparently, sometimes a woman has no choice but to go with him.'

'Are you sorry?'

Lifting her arms over her head, she sunk beneath the water. A second later he felt a playful pull on his big toe.

Bubbles dotted the water before she surfaced. 'No…not yet, at any rate.'

'What would need to happen to make you sorry?'

'A fish nibbling my toes.'

'Trout or pike?'

'I will be sorry if anything living in the water nibbles me.'

Would she really? What if the nibbler didn't actually live in the water? What if—?

But, no…he should not have let the image flash in his mind, let alone nurture the blamed picture of him doing the nibbling.

It was a lucky thing she could not read his mind.

'I think maybe we should go back now. It is rather late,' he said, grateful that he still had that much sense.

With a nod, she swam towards the shore. He stroked after her. When they reached the spot where deep water gave way to the shelf, they waded out.

Chest deep in water, the current surged around

him. He stopped, only now realising the depth of the peril he had landed himself in. Going into the water, he had not given enough thought to what soaked night clothes would reveal coming out of the water.

There were certain things a man should not know about his brother's wife—if Ginny did become that. Even if she did not, there were certain things William was not meant to know.

If he saw her walk on to the shore, her gown clinging to what had to be a sweetly formed body, he would not be able to scour the image from his mind.

'I'm not ready to go back,' he said. 'I'll swim around for a few more minutes.'

'Will, I did not come down to teach you how to beat your brother at skipping stones.'

'And a lucky thing, too.'

She waded a step closer to him. 'I need to ask you…there is something I need to know.'

'Ask me anything. You know you may.'

'I hope I can trust you to give me an honest answer.'

'Always.'

She lifted her face, gazing at the spangle of stars over Lake Ullswater while she spoke.

'Earlier tonight Phillip and I spoke about how your family used to be...he and Cora...and you. How you all got along well and there was no tension in your family. He told me you and Cora got along very well.'

'It is true. She was my sister... I loved her.'

'Would it be the same for us? Your brother thinks so...but, Will, what do you think? Can you accept me as a sister?'

If there were exceptions to always, this was one of them. He would not lie, but neither would he admit to her what he would not even admit to himself.

'Has he declared his intentions to you?' This was the last thing he wanted to know, but blamed if he did not need to know it.

'He has not.'

She turned her gaze upon him, the starlight now lingering in her eyes.

'I need for you to kiss me, Will.'

If a giant fish swam between his legs, carried him across the lake, he could not be more stunned.

No! He would not...could not! Kissing Ginny would betray everyone. Even himself...his sense of honour.

But she touched his cheek, trailing one finger along the line of his jaw. She cupped the back of his neck, went up on her toes. The lift pushed her bosom above the waterline. He did not dare look anywhere but into her eyes. But, no, that was worse. He saw way too much of her heart in her eyes.

'Will...' Her breath warmed his lips, then—

Then she kissed him.

Caught in it, he thought to make it chaste and sweet, but she leaned against his chest where his wet shirt was plastered to his skin. Where her gown and robe were no more than a glistening gossamer smear.

He set her away, calling upon a cavalier smile.

'There, you see?' He hoped his voice sounded nonchalant and not devastated. 'Just like before...proof that we are and will remain friends.'

'You feel you can be my brother?'

'Of course.'

'Good, then...thank you for...'

She looked down, clearly not wanting to meet his gaze. She must have only then noticed the way her wet gown clung to her for she spun away from his gaze. His gaze, which was not focused on her, but a spot over her shoulder. He was not sure what the spot was since it was a blur...everything was a blur.

Only one thing was clear. He had a choice to make...admit to himself what the kiss meant or deny it...to himself and to her.

By confessing that he was shaken by what happened would change his life. Doing so would mean he could not remain here at Hawkwood. He could not live every day, fearing that by a glance or a word he might give his feelings away.

But if he managed to push the draw he felt towards Ginny deep down into his soul where it would never cause harm, he could remain here, be a loyal brother, to both Phillip and to Ginny.

If the time came when he found he could no longer bear it, then he would leave. If he had harboured a doubt that his brother intended to ask Ginny to be his bride, he no longer did.

Surely Phillip would not have spoken to her about fitting into the family, mentioned Cora, had Ginny not been the one to capture his heart.

'Better hurry back to the house. Never know when a pike might get hungry,' he said playfully. He grinned and it hurt.

With that, he turned, stroking away into deep water as if the kiss meant nothing. Worse, as if seeing it meant something to her meant nothing to him.

Only one thing mattered in the end. Phillip's happiness…and that William be a part of it. He desperately wanted to remain at the home he loved…with the people he loved.

Perhaps one day he would take a wife. All four of them would live happily ever after, watching each other's children grow.

And perhaps a giant fish really would surface between his legs and carry him across the lake where just maybe he would escape the sick feeling cramping his gut.

William swam a far distance away without turning to look at her. Ginny knew this because halfway back to the house, she turned to look for him.

Would he turn about? See her and…and nothing.

Let him swim away as if what had happened between them had not. Apparently, he had not felt the lakebed shift when they kissed the way she had.

She was certainly no expert on kissing, but truly, even she recognised that he had responded to her and in a very smouldering way. For her, even the water had begun to steam. But again, she was not an expert. For all she knew this sort of feeling was common to kissing.

If she kissed Phillip it might be the same. How was she to say otherwise? Judging by Will's reaction, such a kiss as they shared was common, experienced and then forgotten.

It was not as though she could ask another woman about it. Perhaps Aunt Adelia…but, no, she would want to know why Ginny was asking and not relent until she knew every detail.

Really, it was not William's fault he did not take to heart the kiss she had forced upon him. Although she had felt him respond, she would bet her journal on it.

'Oh, hang it,' she mumbled.

She had done the boldest thing she could imagine doing. Still, her question had not been answered. No, indeed, it left her more confused than before.

Reaching her room, she closed the door, leaned against it and sighed. There was one more thing she could do.

Kiss Phillip. That would probably answer her question.

Which meant she was not going to have an answer because the last thing she would have the audacity to do was ask the Earl for a kiss to judge his brother's by. The idea of it made her stomach flip.

Deep in thought, she started when she heard her aunt's door open and then close.

How curious. At Cliverton Aunt Adelia was early to bed and early to rise.

The ball was tonight.

If Mother knew William had invited Phillip to ride out with him...challenged him to a race, to put a finer point on it, she would not be pleased.

He and his brother were to be well rested, ready to put their best foot forward, so to speak, and dance the night away.

Would Ginny be ready for it? he wondered. He had considered offering her another dance lesson, but decided it would be too great a risk to his heart...to everyone's heart.

Even thinking about her was too much for him. Last night he had stroked about in the water until he was nearly spent. Then, finding he was not spent enough, he'd run along the shoreline until he was gasping for breath.

Blame it! Even then the touch of Ginny's lips lingered in his mind.

The surprise he had seen in her eyes when he indicated that, for him, the kiss was nothing remarkable...he could not un-see it. He needed to scrub it from his mind. It was why he had issued the challenge of a race to his brother.

'I'll wait for you at the tree.' Phillip laughed, then shifted his weight in the saddle which was his mount's signal to run.

Caught in his thoughts, William had nearly forgotten he was here to beat his brother.

The race was over in under a minute... Phillip the clear winner.

Blame it! Would the man beat him at everything? Even at love?

He would, and by William's own choice.

'Better at racing, better at skipping stones.' Phillip grinned.

Despite William's status as second fiddle, he was grateful to see his brother's smile, to know that his heart was healing.

'How would you feel if I told you I was fond of Ginny?' Phillip asked while they left the river road, walking the horses back to the stables by the smaller path through the woods. 'I know that you like her quite well.'

'I would be glad.' So glad he would endeavour to forget what might have been if things were different.

'Indeed.' His brother gave him a rather curious glance. 'How would you feel if I told you I was fond of Elizabeth?'

'I would be glad, Phillip.' What was he about with these questions? 'I want to see you happy and settled with whichever lady you choose. You do not need my approval if that is what you are after.'

'If I were to make a choice tonight, it would affect you. We will be family...all of us.'

'I know you spoke to Ginny about how it used to be with us...with Cora. I take it this means something?'

'I told her I thought she would fit in well with us. So, yes, that means a great deal.' His brother arched a brow at him as if he were supposed to read something else into the statement. For the life of him, William could not imagine what.

'Did you ask Elizabeth the same thing?'

'No, I hadn't a reason to speak to her of it.'

Again, his brother gave him the look, but with both brows arched.

'Why?' It seemed reasonable that he would have.

'It is something you need to figure out for yourself…but as far as Elizabeth goes, I feel she would also fit nicely into the family.'

'You can hardly wed them both.'

'Indeed not!'

'Winning has gone to your head. You are making no sense.'

For some reason that made his brother laugh, then clap him on the shoulder. 'I am making more sense than you know.'

Ginny sat at her dressing table, watching in the mirror while Aunt Adelia arranged curls in her hair.

It was just as well that all the lady's maids were busy with other guests. Her aunt had such a nice touch with hair and Ginny did want to spend a few moments alone with her.

'What a pretty ribbon,' she commented on the delicate blue satin her aunt twined in and among the strands. 'I do not recall it.'

'No, I do not suppose you would. It is quite old.

It belonged to your mother…or to me depending upon which of us argued the hardest for it on any given day.'

Reaching up, she gently rubbed it between her fingers.

Aunt Adelia squeezed her hand. 'You are going to be the most beautiful woman at the ball, mark my words.'

'I would rather not be, as you well know.'

'Nonsense.' Her aunt gave the hank of hair she had twined on the top of Ginny's head a critical study. 'You have come such a long way. You will shine and enjoy every moment of it.'

Tonight she would be attempting a waltz, so her aunt was too optimistic about the evening. Ginny would need to call upon a great deal of courage to even get through it.

She would begin by having the courage to speak to Aunt Adelia about a subject very much on her mind.

'Auntie, may I ask you something?'

'But of course.'

'It has to do with men…and women.' She took a fortifying breath. 'With men and women together.'

'How delightful. What is it you wish to know?'

'It has to do with kissing.'

'Ah, you no longer wish to go from maiden to marriage without the courtship involved?'

'It would avoid a lot of confusion, if I could.'

'But kissing can be lovely.'

'What I would like to know is if men feel the same emotions about it as women do. Do women take it to heart while men see it as only a pleasant diversion?'

'That can be the case, so a lady must be circumspect about whom she chooses to kiss. But, my dear, when it is right both the gentleman and the lady will take it to heart.'

'So, if only one of the parties takes it to heart it is not to be taken seriously?'

'Why do you ask?' Aunt Adelia gazed at her, tapping her chin in thought. 'Has the Earl kissed you? Did you not feel a spark between you?'

'Lord Hawkwood has been a perfect gentleman. He has not kissed me…it's only that I wonder…in case he does.'

'I see.' Ginny had a niggling suspicion that her aunt really did see. 'If he does kiss you…if any gentleman does, you ought to feel a delightful tingle. If you do not, then the gentleman might not be meant for you.'

'Thank you, Auntie. I just wanted to be sure.'

'Now stand up and let me see you.'

Rising from the chair, she turned slowly in a circle so Aunt Adelia could judge the results of her work.

The truth was, she did feel rather lovely in her shimmering blue gown. It felt as though she was wearing the sky…or the lake. Earrings sparkled on her earlobes as if she was stepping among stars.

The ribbon made her feel a connection to her mama.

'As far as kissing goes, you had better be vigilant, Ginny.' Her aunt shot her a playful wink. 'There will not be a man in attendance who will not want to kiss you. I would not even rule out Lord Smythe, who you know is completely smitten with Mary.'

'Heaven help me. You know looking this way will make me appear even more of a fool on the dance floor. Ladies are supposed to be graceful.'

'You have been taking lessons, I believe?' Her aunt gave her a thoughtful look. 'Surely William has helped you to improve your skills?'

'Yes, he has been giving me lessons. Truly,

Auntie, he has been the soul of patience, but I have improved very little.'

'I don't believe it.' Aunt Adelia seemed overly optimistic about her skills. 'Come then, let us go down and put William's instructions to the test.'

Chapter Twelve

William stood beside his mother in the hall, greeting the last of the guests.

'It looks like rain again,' she noted while peering out of the open doors. 'Ah, here comes Bishop Stevens.'

And not a moment too soon.

Judging by the way the weather cooled so dramatically and the wind gusted into the hall, rustling his trouser legs and the hem of Mother's gown, it might be a lot of rain.

'You invited the Bishop to the ball?'

'This is not just any ball, as you know. Phillip might make his choice tonight. It is only right that the Bishop be here. He has been with us in our most sorrowful times and it is only right that he rejoice with us as well.'

'Phillip might not make his choice tonight.'
But he very well might.

'In the event, it has been some time since we have seen him and we will enjoy his company.'

It was true. Bishop Stevens was close to the family, both friend and clergyman. He had baptized both him and Phillip. If an engagement was announced he ought to be here for it.

'I hear the orchestra, William. Run along and make yourself useful with the ladies.'

'As always, Mother, your wish is my command.'

'You know you adore dancing.' Her lips twitched at the corners, a gesture he understood to be an indulgent smile.

'Did you save a spot for me on your dance card?'

'Scamp.' She shooed her fingers at him.

'I mean it… Father would dance with you if he were here. I would like to twirl you about in his stead.'

'I no longer twirl about…but perhaps I will let you lead me sedately around the room.'

He kissed her cheek, then turned to go.

'And one more thing, William. Make sure Lady Ginny dances with Phillip.'

He nodded, then walked towards the ballroom.

After all the time he had spent helping Ginny

get ready to dance with his brother, the validation of his instruction was about to be put on display.

He was not sure if he was more anxious to see the result of his tutelage or more nervous.

She would shine, he knew that...but she would also be taking a risk.

It would break his heart to see her step expectantly into Phillip's arms and then watch her stumble over her slippers or trip over his brother's long foot.

Perhaps he could find a way to keep her away from Phillip's invitation until the last when people were weary of dancing and sought other entertainment.

Coming into the ballroom, he did not see Ginny. Glancing about, he did spot a circle of young men, their attention consumed by a lady standing at the centre of their orbit.

Only one woman he knew had hair that colour—the self-same woman who would not enjoy being the object of their admiration.

He did not doubt that every one of the gentlemen was trying to win the honour of escorting the blue-gowned angel about the dance floor.

Lady Della waved her hand, trying to catch

his attention, but he pretended not to notice. He stepped quickly towards the wall of garden doors where Ginny fended off her admirers.

Some of the ladies appeared annoyed at the men's attention towards Ginny. Their envy was obvious by their frowns and by the whispers behind their hands.

In William's opinion they had good reason to be envious. Ginny Penneyjons, wearing a gown that looked like blue moonlight and a ribbon in her hair which matched the colour of her eyes, was luminous.

Elizabeth smiled while she waltzed with Phillip. His brother seemed as happy to be dancing with Elizabeth as she did with him. Since his brother was the Earl, it was his job to make people feel good.

Yet there had been the odd conversation with his brother this morning where it had seemed he was partial to both Ginny and Elizabeth. Even now he could not work out what that had been about. Phillip was the least fickle person he knew. Shrugging the puzzlement of it away, he turned his attention back to Ginny.

'Good evening, Lady Ginny,' he said while

elbowing his way into the circle of gents. 'You look exceptionally pretty tonight.'

Knowing Ginny, she was past weary of hearing the compliment, but it was the thing to say and he did mean it.

'Have you had a chance to eat anything?'

'I have been so engaged chatting with these charming gentlemen that eating has not crossed my mind.'

'Now that it has, would you do me the honour of joining me for something to eat?'

She placed her hand in the crook of his elbow, smiling. It touched him, somehow, to know that he was the only man who knew her well enough to recognise that her smile was one of relief.

He doubted even Phillip would know that when her lips pursed just so, tipping the tiniest bit down at one corner, it was a gesture of relief.

How long would it be before Phillip knew things about her that he did not?

While he might be escorting Ginny to the dining room, he had lost his appetite.

'Thank you. I am quite hungry after all.'

Entering the buffet room, they approached a table laden with delectable food. The talent of those who worked in the kitchen was spoken of in Ullswater and beyond.

William offered Ginny a plate and took one for himself. Too bad he did not feel like eating.

'What can I get for you?' he asked.

'I could not eat if I tried. But you must... I'll wait here with you while you do.'

He set both plates down on the table.

While he had no appetite for food, gazing at the woman beside him, he found he was hungry after all...for her.

Pretending he did not want to kiss her was futile. While he struggled to get his emotions under control, Phillip came into the room.

'There you are, Ginny!'

William's heart took a hard kick as he saw his brother's grin. There had been a time when he despaired of ever seeing it again. Until this moment he had not realised it was possible to be overjoyed and despairing at the same time.

How was he going to live with his heart sliced down the middle? It was bleeding and he feared he would not be able to hide the wound.

In order to wrap a symbolic bandage on it, he plucked up something to eat. He popped it into his mouth without paying attention to what it was. Chewed and smiled as if he enjoyed it.

'Will you dance with me before the other fellows wear out your slippers?'

Ginny's test was upon her. William's heart skipped, then stuttered. He wished he could keep her from the ordeal. But this was what he had been preparing her for, was it not?

'I cannot think of anything I would enjoy more.'

Her smile appeared genuine, but she did cast William a glance before going out of the room.

Walking out behind them, he tried to hear what they were saying, but with the merry sounds of the ball going on, he could not.

The one thing he did hear clearly was Phillip laughing.

Good. The more his brother laughed the more it indicated his healing. It was what William wanted more than anything.

William should probably find a lady wishing to dance. It was his job to keep the guests entertained.

But, no. There would be time for that later. He was going to stand with his back pressed against the closed garden door, watch and pray this dance would go well.

He was dimly aware that wind-driven rain pattered the glass behind him. 'Please let her do well.' He moved his lips, but made no sound.

Even with people watching, Ginny smiled while Phillip led her to the centre of the floor. She was off to an excellent start. As Countess, she would need to get used to being watched. The Earl was always under scrutiny—as his wife she would be as well.

Playing second fiddle might be the hardest thing William had ever done. Indeed...who had made such an observation? Ah, yes...he remembered now, it was a reverend, Charles Spurgeon.

'It needs more skill than I can tell. To play the second fiddle well.' He whispered the truth under his breath...twice.

This was Ginny's moment to shine or fall. All he could do was stand here in the background and hope what he taught her let her sparkle... for Phillip.

He had played his part and now he would watch, his heart cupped in his hands while the graceful moves he had taught her further won his brother's heart.

Or, she could trip and be humiliated.

Whatever it was he had eaten sat like a great lump in his belly. 'Please let her do well,' he prayed again, this time in a whisper.

'She will, of course.'

Caught up in his thoughts, he had failed to notice Aunt Adelia come up beside him.

'I understand she has been under your tutelage.'

'Yes, but briefly, of course.'

'I thank you for that... I imagine you know how she hates being the centre of attention. If she fails at this, she will be crushed.'

'My brother will not let that happen.' He hoped. 'He is skilled at making other people look good.'

'Of course, we all have our skills. It must be difficult for you to stand by and not have anyone know that it is you who ought to take the credit if she manages this.'

'Ginny will know.' And no one else needed to.

The orchestra began a waltz. Phillip caught Ginny up in the stance, his hand pressing the small of her back, her hand resting on his upper arm.

They moved.

One, two, three...one, two, three...he counted

off the rhythmic pattern in his mind as if some-how it would help.

Good, no misstep so far. But here came a twirl...he sucked in his breath. Ginny's toe brushed Phillip's boot, but the misstep was slight and not noticeable.

Come on, Ginny, he thought, clenching his fists. His stomach roiled...*you can do this*! By rights, he should be showing her off, whirling her about with pride in her accomplishments.

Since that was not to be, he stood by the doors next to Aunt Adelia, imaging it was him.

They twirled about the ballroom. When Phillip and Ginny passed the spot where he and Aunt Adelia stood, he saw she was smiling.

If she knew William was watching it did not show, her attention was all for his brother...as it should be.

And then it happened.

Her step went wide, caught Phillip's trouser leg. She fell towards him.

William would never know how it happened for sure, but in catching her, his brother managed to make the fall look as though it was his fault... as if it was his foot which tangled in her skirt.

Phillip laughed out loud, declaring how sorry he was.

And then Elizabeth, who was as skilled a dancer as any William had ever seen, managed to trip and fall towards her partner in the same way Ginny had fallen into Phillip. She and her partner started to laugh.

Incredibly…the fall caught on…as if it were some new and bizarre step to the waltz. Ladies all around fell into their partners' arms.

The orchestra played on, everyone laughing while resuming the dance. Everyone but William.

Phillip led Ginny towards the banquet room. William heard them still laughing over what had happened. Perhaps with the danger of the dance over and having come through it without humiliation, Ginny's appetite was restored.

Not so for William. What he had believed to be unique between him and Ginny, the laughter which sprang between them as easily as breathing, perhaps was not as singular as he assumed.

'My word, William, your brother is skilled.'

'He has been trained in social matters since he was a tot.'

'Is that what we witnessed just now…social

manoeuvring?' Adelia looked at him thoughtfully and for once without a smile. 'Or was it a bit more intimate? What do you think? Will they suit each other? Do they have that special heart bond?'

'I'm not one to judge my brother's heart.'

'No, I imagine not...but how do you judge your own heart, my boy?'

Loyal, but miserable? Traitorous, but resigned? Both of those, but he could not admit to her. He should not even think it in the presence of this perceptive woman.

'I could not be happier for them,' was what he answered, which was not a lie. And yet not the truth, either.

'Perhaps it is for the best that when you kissed her you felt nothing special...no spark...no tingle.'

'She told you that?' Where was the hole he could dive into?

'Well, she never said it was you...but I suspected so. But since you seem to be happy with your brother's and Ginny's relationship, I can only assume it is true...that you did not feel the attraction.' She patted his cheek. 'No matter, I suppose, since there are any one of several ladies present you might spark things up with. Oh…there is Lord Helm just come in. Goodnight, my dear.'

'No spark,' William muttered to himself while he opened the patio doors, stepped outside, then closed them behind him.

Rain hit the stone in a rhythmic splat. He made a dash for the gazebo which lay twenty yards around the bend of a gravel pathway.

No spark…what had that been if not a spark? A blaze was what and nothing less. He only pretended to feel nothing because…

Why?

Inside the cosy garden room, he closed the door then lit a lantern which was kept on a small table between a pair of stuffed chairs.

Standing at the window, staring out, all he saw was his own reflection. His image reflected misery. Why?

Because he loved his brother. Because he loved Ginny. Because they probably loved each other.

A situation which was not the end of the world.

All he needed to do to remain in the home he loved, with the people he loved, was make sure his affection for Ginny was brotherly.

Surely he could commit to that much. Love was love, no matter what one called it. Familial love, romantic love, brotherly love…were they such different things?

Perhaps last night at the lake he was caught up in the moment. Yes, thinking about it, his reaction might have had to do with being flattered that a woman like Ginny wanted to kiss him.

The steamy and yet sweetly innocent kiss had made him feel grand. Surely one kiss did not mean he could not love Ginny in an appropriate way. The love of a brother for a sister was better than not being able to love her at all.

Accepting the situation for what it was would be far better than never seeing her again. Perhaps if he kissed her again he would not feel a spark. How could he if her spark were for Phillip?

It all made sense…so logical he nearly sighed in relief, but only nearly because there was still that nagging voice which suggested he was selling himself a lie. Perhaps he was doing that… but it was a lie he could live with. A lie he would live with.

For the sake of everyone he would live with it.

Hearing steps crunching on gravel, he squinted

past raindrops dripping down the glass, but could not identify who was out there.

The doorknob turned.

Ginny rushed inside, blinking water off her lashes. 'Oh, good,' she gasped. 'I found you.'

'You were looking for me?'

Why? Could it mean that she was not having a happy time with his brother...perhaps not hearing a declaration of his intentions towards her?

He did not dare to think it.

'Who else would I be looking for right now, Will?'

'I thought you would be with Phillip.' Live with it...live with it and be grateful. 'The two of you looked good dancing together.'

'Yes, only thanks to you.' She took his hand, squeezing it. 'I was a little nervous at first with everyone watching. But I counted out the steps like you taught me to, then I felt the music and then your brother just whisked me away in the fun of it.'

She dropped his hand, stretched her arms out to her sides and spun about as if living the moment again in her mind. She stopped suddenly, her damp hem sagging at her ankles.

'But then my foot caught in his trouser leg.' He

was glad to see she could smile about it. 'And do you know what, Will? It was not the end of the world.'

'As far as I can tell, it caused a great deal of merriment.'

'Yes, but everyone thought it was Phillip who tripped. And then it was Elizabeth who really saved the moment.'

She laughed. Why could he not laugh with her?

When he ought to be rejoicing for her having accomplished the dance, he simply stared at her mouth with non-fraternal thoughts scurrying about his mind…with disloyal longings racing through his blood and threatening his brotherly intentions.

If he was going to manage to live a lie, he had to know if it was even possible to do. Lusting after his brother's wife would be a great sin. Given the way he felt, wishing he could kiss the curve of her smile, feel her sweet, feminine heat on his lips…the rise and fall of her breathing under his fingers…and her heartbeat—

For all his brotherly intentions, he had grave doubts that he would live up to them. It would be better to go away than to live with wanting Ginny every day and she his brother's wife.

'You ought to be with Phillip, celebrating your survival of the waltz.'

'He is not the one who knows what it took for me to give it a try.' She shook her head. Her frown creased delicate lines at the corners of her eyes. 'No, Will. It is no celebration unless it is with you.'

And perhaps there was no life here at Hawkwood unless it was with Ginny. Not Phillip and Ginny… William and Ginny.

'Has my brother spoken to you of his intentions yet?'

'No, Will.'

Were those remnants of raindrops glistening in her eyes or something else?

Blame it! Was it Phillip's lack of decisiveness which caused her sadness? But in fairness who could be expected to make such a decision in such a short time?

You could, whispered the inconvenient voice in his head. Didn't it know he could not since the choice was not his to make?

'He only wants to be certain before he speaks.

Not certain about how he feels, I don't think…
but about how you feel.'

How did she feel? The question sat uneasy on
his heart. Good Lord help him…how did he want
her to feel? Did he want this woman at the cost
of his brother's happiness? Could he live with
the guilt of it? Could he live without her?

Perhaps, if she did not feel for him what he felt
for her. But he suspected she might, way down
in his gut he wondered. He greatly feared what
he imagined he saw in her eyes. There was but
one way to know the truth of it, a way that spoke
what words could not.

Ginny was leaning back against the gazebo
door. Rain and wind lashed hard on the glass behind her. She must be frightened of the weather
and yet she had come out in it to find him.

He stepped close to her…quite close…too
close. Over steady rain pelting the gazebo, he
heard the quick whisper of her breath. It took
his away, snatched it cleanly out of his lungs.

'Your aunt told me there was no spark when
we kissed. Was it true, Ginny? For you?'

He dipped his head, she lifted her face.

She touched his cheek, drew his mouth down
upon hers…slowly, gently…and then—

There was a spark. It ignited a flame which burst suddenly into a sensation that felt like erupting fireworks. It was as if colour burst all around, bolted from his fingertips and set his heart on fire.

Leaning away from the door, she pressed against him. He slid one arm about her waist to press her perfect curves closer, to breathe in her scent and hear the half-stifled moan whispering under his kiss.

This was it, then. The answer he'd been seeking…dreading. With the greatest effort of his life he set her away from him.

'I guess your aunt was right, then,' he muttered, feeling sick with the lie.

She blinked at him, confusion marking her eyes and the turn of her lips.

Even so, the last thing he was going to admit was being in love with his brother's probable intended. With nothing but naked emotion raging through him, he could no longer deny the truth. The truth being that he loved Ginny. Not as a sister, as a man. There was no going back from it.

He did not dare to even look into her eyes. The last thing he wanted was for her to see his bared soul…his sliced and bleeding heart. There was but one thing for him to do—go away, from everyone and everything he loved.

Ginny spun about, opened the door and dashed out into the rain without closing it.

He watched her run down the path, listening to the crunch of her slippers…committing to memory the way she moved. She lifted her hand towards her face, whisking something off her cheek. Rain or tears, he would never know.

What he did know was that the moisture dampening his face was not caused by the gust blowing in the doorway.

Chapter Thirteen

Ginny ran through the rain, her slippers soaked, her cheeks damp with tears. How could she have been so mistaken about Will's kiss…again? The same as before, she gave herself over to it…to him. At that moment, had he asked her to do anything…anything…she would have done it.

But he hadn't asked her. Except to believe that his kisses were meaningless. Nothing more than casual flirtation…a game.

Dashing up the patio steps, she decided not to enter through the ballroom. The last thing she wanted was for anyone to see her wet and weeping. She would never be able to explain why. She did not know why…except that Will did not feel what she did.

Making her way along the side of the house, she went towards the solarium where she could enter with no one likely to see her. She was more confused than she had ever been in her life.

According to Aunt Adelia's assessment of what made for a good marriage, she and Will were not meant to be. In order to have a true marriage, there must be a spark...a tingle. Oh, it had been there for her, setting all her parts ablaze...but once again, not for him.

What she needed to do was kiss someone else to discover if it was common for women to become hot and bothered, and for men to not.

Phillip. She could trust him to give her an honest answer. The last thing she wanted to do was ask him that favour. But she needed an answer and who better to set her straight on it?

This was going to take some courage. She would gather what she had, ask him for a kiss and discover if either of them was moved by it. If he, too, did not feel anything, then perhaps she was destined to live as a spinster after all, which was going to be a harder thing to do than if she had never kissed William and felt her world fall in, and out, of place.

But first she would need to dry off. She did not want Phillip or anyone asking why she had gone out in the rain. She crossed the solarium and was sneaking down the hallway when she heard a voice.

'Ginny!' Elizabeth hurried towards her. 'Why are you wet?'

'Because I am on my way to put on dry clothes and I have not yet reached my chamber.'

'How did you get that way in the first place?'

'I went for a walk...looking for Lord Hawkwood.'

'He is in the library. You might have saved yourself some trouble had you checked in the house first.'

It was hard to know for sure in the dim light of the hallway, but she thought Elizabeth's cheeks were flushed.

'Thank you for what you did, Elizabeth.'

'What I did?' Indeed, her friend was blushing.

'During the waltz...when you turned my fall into fun.'

'But it was fun!' Elizabeth shrugged, waggling her dance card. 'I must hurry back.'

And Ginny must hurry to the library before she lost her courage, the state of her gown be hanged.

The library door was open so she knocked on the frame. Going inside, she found Phillip standing beside the fireplace, shrugging his arms into his coat.

'Ginny?' He gave her a quick glance, head to toe. He could not fail to notice she was rather damp. 'Had I realised you wanted to go out, I would have found you an umbrella.'

'Had I been thinking more clearly I would not have gone out at all.'

'You did leave me rather suddenly…you didn't eat a bite before you rushed out of the buffet room.'

'I needed to speak with someone.'

'Let me guess… William?'

'Did you know he was trying to teach me to dance? So that just maybe I would not humiliate myself when the time came to dance with you.'

'Yes, I was aware. I saw the two of you on the dock…practising. You did very well tonight until the mishap.'

'Mishap is a kind way of describing my clumsiness. Had it not been for you, the dance would have ended in disaster.'

'Shall we go back to the ballroom and try it again?'

'I think I would rather go back out in the rain.'

She would also rather do that than ask him

what she had come to ask. But do it she would. If she could not trust Phillip to set her straight on how men felt about kissing, she did not know whom she could trust.

Phillip was comfortable to be around and she had come to value his companionship. Except for Will, she could not recall a man's company she enjoyed more.

She thought she could ask him anything…she was about to find out if this was true.

'Well, I have come here to ask something of you…a favour.'

'Certainly, Ginny. What can I do?'

'Kiss me.'

Perhaps she ought to have led up to the unusual request. He did look rather stunned.

'I mean, if it is not too awkward.'

'What sort of kiss do you have in mind?'

'The usual sort…but I imagine I should explain…and do not feel you must oblige me.'

'Any man would count himself lucky to be asked for a kiss by you, Ginny.'

Not any man…not the man who mattered.

But she was here to discover the truth and to do so, she must not think of William Talton.

Imagining him while kissing Phillip would not give her an accurate reading of the act.

'You see my aunt says there ought to be delightful tingles when one kisses a man and I would like to know if it is true.'

'Hmph…as I said, there are many kinds of kisses. Some appropriate for one circumstance and other kinds for another. Shall I give you the one that is from my heart…for I do care for you very deeply.'

'Yes…from your heart, please, Phillip.'

She closed her eyes, felt his fingers on her chin. Gently, he turned her face, kissed her cheek.

'Tingles?' His hand fell away…a smile stretched his mouth.

'No…not a single one.'

'It was different when my brother kissed you, I imagine.'

'What makes you think he did?'

'You do…surely it is not my kiss that has you blushing.'

One would think discussing something so personal would be difficult, but for some reason, with Phillip it was not.

'Yes, then, he did. More than once and he felt nothing. While I…well…'

'Why do you think he did not feel anything?'

'He told me.'

'He was lying, then.' He took her by the hand, led her to the couch. 'Let's sit and discuss this.'

'All right…although I cannot imagine why he would lie about it.'

They sat on the couch, turning so that they spoke face to face.

'It's my fault, really.' He scrubbed his hand over his face, then shook his head. 'I might have led him to believe that my tender feelings towards you were of a different nature than they are.'

'I cannot understand why you would do that.'

'Of course you can. Anyone can see how it is between the two of you, how it been from the beginning…from ten years ago if you care to go back that far. I only thought that by making him jealous, it would push him towards you.'

'Oh, well… I do not think he is.'

'I'm sorry, Ginny. It seems I pushed him away instead. I did not take into account my brother's loyal nature. Honestly, it only now occurs to me that he must consider his feelings for you to be a betrayal of me.'

'But, Phillip…you say anyone could see how

things are between me and William. I cannot see it. I doubt he feels any differently towards me than he does any of the other ladies here.'

'Ginny, you know that isn't true. My brother is friendly and so he treats everyone with consideration. Do not mistake his attentions towards them as being the same as for you. If he has not told you how he feels, it is not because of his feelings for other women, it is because of his love for me.'

Thunder boomed against the library windows. Last time that had happened in this room she had leapt into Will's arms…and he'd kissed her.

'My brother is in love with you.' He reached for her hand, squeezed it. 'I think you know it… in your heart you do.'

'He's never indicated so.'

'Only because he believes I wish to make my declaration to you…and I do have one, just not what my fool brother thinks it is. But here it is… I truly do love you, Ginny. I would like nothing more than to become your brother-in-law.'

'In that case I think I will not have my question about passionate kisses answered by you.'

'Come.' He stood, bringing her up with him. 'We shall find my brother and let him answer it.'

'If he will,' she said, walking beside him and going out of the room.

'Oh, once I explain things, he will be eager enough. Do you trust me on it?'

'I trust that you believe it, at least.'

He laughed, which for some reason made her feel much better about things.

'You kissed Elizabeth before I came in, didn't you?'

'Indeed, I did…and there were tingles.'

What wonderful news!

'I'm happy to hear it. Elizabeth was fond of you from the first night.'

'I was confused on the first night. But let's go find my brother and put your uncertainty to rest.'

'How can you be so sure he feels what I feel for him?'

'I know him. Trust me. He is about to become the happiest man in the world.'

'Your mother will not be happy, nor my aunt,' she admitted while he led her through the solarium. 'They set up this whole country house visit just to match you and me up, you can be sure they did.'

At the door, Phillip handed her an umbrella and snatched one up for himself.

'It's understandable. They have been the best of friends since they were children. What could be better for them than to have their families joined? As soon as we inform William how mis-directed his loyalty is, I have no doubt they will get what they want.'

Ginny's stomach felt upside down. If Phillip was correct in what he believed, why hadn't William revealed how he felt?

There was every chance that she was about to have her heart shattered.

'I'll tell you the truth, Ginny—this time last year I was a broken man. William saw my grief…he lived it. He would not be who he is if he did not put what he thought to be my well-being ahead of his. He will even deny his feelings for you because of it…but not for ever.'

'Where are we going?'

'Normally he'd go down to the water when he's got something on his mind. Since it's rain-ing, he's probably in the stable. He also likes to go to the loft when he's brooding over a matter.'

It was a long dash to the stable, but she was not too wet because of the umbrella.

The light was dim as they entered, but there

were a pair of lamps burning. Glancing about, she did not see Will.

Horses whickered, the air inside smelled like fresh hay, damp with cool, moist air.

'William?' Phillip called, then hurried up the loft ladder. Shaking his head, he came back down. 'He's not up there.'

'Perhaps he is back in the ballroom?'

'Lord Hawkwood!' The stableman stepped out from a stall. 'Your brother has gone.'

'Gone? In this weather? Did he say where to?'

'He gave me a message to deliver to you. He said I was to relay it in the morning, but here you are and your brother did not seem himself. Shall I tell you now?'

Gone? She clutched Phillip's arm.

'Now, please, Mr Flynn,' he answered, covering her fingers and giving them a squeeze.

'He says to tell you that he wishes you and Lady Ginny well. He could not be happier for you.' Mr Flynn nodded at her, unsmiling. 'May I say, sir...he did not look sincere about it?'

'Did he tell you where he was going?'

'No, but he did speak a bit to his horse while he was readying to go... I couldn't help but overhear. Told the beast he was going back to the sea.'

'In the middle of the night?' Ginny gasped. 'In this weather?'

'I did suggest he wait until morning, my lady, but he was that set on going at once.'

'I imagine he intends to go to Liverpool, probably by way of Whitehaven,' Phillip said.

Ginny thought he might have cursed under his breath even though it would be unlike him to do so.

'Mr Flynn, will you prepare the carriage for travel?'

'Of course, my lord. Look for it within thirty minutes.'

Taking Ginny by the elbow, he escorted her back to the house. He turned to her at the foot of the backstairs, his formal wear dripping.

'I'll bring him back to you. I promise.'

'But, no… I'm going with you.'

He was going to forbid her. She saw the decree forming in his mind. As Hawkwood he could decree it.

And she could ignore it.

Ginny was changed and ready for travel within ten minutes. She ought to let Aunt Adelia know what she was doing, but since she was sneaking away, she could not.

Running for the stable under the shelter of an umbrella, she wondered if she could do what she set her mind to. Was she that bold?

But ride out in a storm? With thunder and lightning crashing all about?

Lady Admirable had done it on occasion and the fictional character had sprung from Ginny's mind. So, yes, she must be able.

Hopefully the horse would be braver than she was.

Dashing into the stable, she spotted Mr Flynn preparing the carriage.

'Lord Hawkwood has requested an extra horse,' she lied…but for the best of causes.

'I mean no disrespect, my lady, but why has he sent you to ask?'

Why?

'As anxious as I am to bring Lord Hawkwood's brother home, I am set and ready to travel. Since I am first here I said I would relay the message. No need to send anyone out in the weather when I am here already.'

'I was going to bring the carriage around.'

'Of course…but here I am. If you will please saddle a good steady horse, I would be grateful.'

She gave him a winsome, pleading smile.

'Yes, of course. I would be happy to.'

Beauty did have its purpose upon occasion, she supposed.

'Please, if you would, let my lord know that I have put rain gear in the saddle pack.'

Oh…she was more grateful to hear that than he could know.

'Have you an extra tarp, as well? To cover the horse when we stop?'

'Indeed, I was about to bring one.'

He went into the tack room.

Which gave her just the time she needed to lead the horse outside, to mount and trot away.

Chapter Fourteen

A mile up the road lightning struck the top of a cedar. While William spoke calming words to his horse, he watched the trunk split down the middle.

With a violent crash, half of the tree fell across the road. He listened to it hiss while being pelted by heavy rain, watched steam rise into the air.

If the Good Lord was trying to tell him to turn back, that he had made a hasty and unwise decision, this was a dramatic way to do it. At the very least he figured it suggested he ought to take shelter until morning.

But where? He glanced about. Since he had not made it terribly far from home, he knew the area. Dismounting, he led the horse off the road towards a cave he thought he remembered being close by. There was no point in pushing his mount through the mess and risk injuring him.

It took a while to reach it, but it was close to where he expected it to be. Going inside, he was beyond grateful to be out of wet, lashing wind.

The cave was a snug fit, but blessedly dry. Someone must use the shelter on occasion because it contained a neat stack of firewood, along with kindling and matches.

After tending to the horse, he lit a fire near the entrance and then sat down. He leaned against the rock wall, closed his eyes and waited for morning.

Looking at things now, it was clear that his decision to leave so quickly had been impulsive…highly unwise. Even had it not been raining, what kind of fool set out on a journey in the dark of night?

His kind of fool.

A heartbroken fool.

He cursed out loud since the horse would not be offended. Indeed, there was some satisfaction in hearing the rude word echo off the walls.

In the end, the outburst changed nothing.

He was in love with his brother's future wife. There had been no choice but to go away because there would come a time when he would no longer be able to hide his feelings for Ginny.

The last thing he was going to do was tear his family apart.

What were they doing now? Making the happy announcement…celebrating? The picture of it bloomed in his mind. It hurt to see, but he could not look away. Mother and Aunt Adelia would be mad with joy, weeping with it, no doubt.

He ought to have said something about his feelings from the start. If only he'd had the courage to tell Phillip how he felt, he might not be sitting in a dark cave with a damp, smelly horse his only company. He might not be sick at heart, fearing he had left his life behind him.

He had not spoken for the best of reasons. Phillip's well-being meant everything to him. He would not do anything that might send him back to the dark state he had been in. He could cling to that reasoning if he wished to because it was the truth.

But the still small voice in his head, which had an annoying way of intruding when he did not wish to hear it, spoke up, telling him there was more to the truth than that. There was a bond between him and Ginny. On his half of it was love, not as a brother for a sister as he had led her to believe, but as a man for a woman…a husband for a wife.

He stood up, pacing a circle around the horse when the voice persisted. If Ginny did feel for him what he felt for her—and it was not impossible, in his heart he knew it—then he had done his brother a great disservice.

Phillip wanted a marriage like the one he had shared with Cora. Cora never spent a single day of their marriage with a divided heart. She loved Phillip and no other…no questions…no doubts or shadows.

Thinking about it made him feel gut kicked, as if his placid animal had lifted his hoof and hit him square in the belly.

Ginny would not have asked him to kiss her if she had given her heart to his brother. He knew her better than to believe she would. Now that he faced the truth of it, he understood that Ginny was not the bride for Phillip. The marriage would be doomed from the start. And it would be his fault because he had been too much a fool to reveal what was in his heart.

Coward, or fool? the voice poked.

A coward would keep what he knew to himself, fearing what might come of his honesty.

A fool would continue along to Whitehaven. He would go back to sea and hide behind the lie that this was best for everyone.

Could he do it? Betray Phillip, Ginny and himself?

Blame it! He did not wish to be a coward any more than he did a fool. Until this moment he had counted his own desires as unworthy of consideration. Looked at in the hard light of truth, admitting his love for Ginny was not selfish. No! By failing to do so, he might condemn them all.

Sitting back down, he rested his arms on bent knees, rested his head on his wrists.

He had a decision to wrestle with. Chances were he would be arguing the right and wrong of it all night long.

A tree blocked the road. It must have been felled by lightning. It looked rather ghostly, steaming and hissing with rain hitting it. Was that the fate she and her brave horse would meet? She shivered, then led the horse around it.

Where was Will?

Anything might have happened to him. Her mind offered many pictures, all of them dastardly. Her visons shifted from seeing him fallen off his horse, his leg broken…or fallen off his horse and drowned in a puddle…or wet and sick. Or, if he had not been struck by wicked lightning, having boarded a ship. Her mind even supplied a couple of smitten ladies who were enchanted by his dimples, waving while he sailed away from the dock.

Or, he might have had the wisdom to turn back, which was more than she had. If there was any chance he was out there, getting further away from her every minute, she was not going back.

Oh, she was frightened of the weather, she had not stopped shivering since she set out. The thing of it was, she was more frightened of living her life without Will.

She needed to press on with as much haste as was safe for her mount. No doubt when they discovered she had gone, someone would come after her. At least if they did it would probably be in a carriage which was bound to slow them down. They would want to put her some place safe the instant they spotted her.

Even if they tried, she would not meekly sit inside where it was safe. Was that not what she had done all her life? Stood in the shadows where life seemed safe?

Hearing thunder roll overhead, she shivered, but she also straightened in the saddle because she was exceedingly proud of herself. She was going after the man she loved, no matter where the perilous path might lead. Whether he accepted her love or rejected it, she would deal with it when it came.

For now she huddled under the rain gear and— 'Stop,' she said to the horse. What was that in the hillside? A fire...in a cave! It glowed quite cheerily about halfway up the hillside.

It must be Will! It only stood to reason he would seek shelter. She prayed quite desperately it was him and not a stranger sitting beside the fire.

The rock wall behind him pressed uncomfortably on his back, but the fire glow...if he closed his eyes he could imagine he was home.

He did not dare close them because whenever he did, his mind supplied a vision of Ginny. Not of her cooing to a duckling, not of her dancing happily with Phillip, either. His vision presented an image of her face, how crushed she appeared when he callously lied and led her to believe there was nothing special about their kiss.

Nothing could be more of a lie. Four times he'd kissed her. Four times it had rocked him to his toes. Even…no, especially the one when he had kissed her forehead, then vowed to find her and marry her. Ever since, she had been there, a secret and tender glow in his heart.

There was one reason he had never married. Looking at it now, he knew it had nothing to do with fearing loss. No one had ever been his Ginny, that was the plain fact of it. His Ginny… not Phillip's Ginny.

How long would he sit here in this cave, believing that, for as much as he loved Phillip, his own feelings did not count for anything? That Ginny's feelings did not count. Not another minute was how long.

'We are leaving,' he announced to the horse while bounding to his feet. He bent to pick up the saddle, lifting it halfway to the horse's back.

'Can you wait until morning, Will? I'm rather cold.'

He was unaware that he had dropped the saddle until it pinched his toe. But pain was good.

It meant he was not asleep and dreaming Ginny stood at the cave entrance, dripping and holding the reins of an equally dripping horse.

The beast was the first to move. It shoved past him to join the other horse at the rear of the cave while William stood as if struck dumb.

What was she doing here?

'I've come to bring you home, Will,' she answered the question he had not asked. 'But I guess you have made up your mind to go to sea. I've come too late.' Her hair dripped, her eyes dripped and her chin trembled.

And he was undone, completely and irrevocably.

'Ginny...' He reached for her, drawing the raincoat off. 'Are you here alone? Where is my brother?'

'I came alone.'

'In a storm?' He could still not believe she was standing here so close he could hear her breathing. 'Why would you take such a risk? You must be terrified.'

She nodded, shivering. He folded her up in his arms.

'Ginny,' he whispered against her hair. 'There is something I must say.'

'If you tell me to go home, I will not. I will sit here by the fire until the storm passes.'

'I need you to kiss me, Ginny.'

'Why?'

'To prove me a liar.'

'But why—?'

He cupped her chin, lifted her face. 'Kiss...'

Up on her toes, she wrapped her arms around the back of his neck. He hugged her about the waist and lifted her off her feet.

Her kiss was not sweet, not demure. It was possessive, she lay claim to his heart and he gladly handed it over. His kiss was hot passion, he meant to capture her...felt it when she gave herself to him.

'There is the truth,' he breathed against her lips. 'It has always been the truth.'

He set her down, but kissed her again just to be sure this was real. When he pulled away, she yanked him back for another.

'You felt a tingle? Both times?' she asked.

'I always did.' Taking her hand, he drew her down to sit by the fire. 'I'm sorry I lied about it. I hope I'm not too late... Have you committed to my brother?'

'Does it seem as though I have? Really, Will—'

He kissed her again, a long and lingering kiss which made him think she was not likely to still be cold.

'Just making sure,' he said and felt his grin stretch to the limits of his face. 'Why didn't you, though?'

'I came through a storm to get to you, risking life and limb. Why would I, do you think? Not because I accepted Phillip's proposal and came to inform you of it!'

'You turned him down, Ginny? But he's an earl!'

'What he is not is the man I love, Will.' She touched his cheek, trailed her warm finger down his cheek, stroked the curve of his bottom lip. 'You are and I think you know it.'

'I hear you…and I do know it, but I can scarcely let myself believe it. I've spent a great deal of effort denying it could be possible for us, you understand.'

'I do understand it, Will…loving your brother as you do, you would never do anything to endanger his happiness.' Her smile might have been the most heart-warming sight he had ever seen. 'I promise you, you have not. He is not in love with me…but I believe he is with someone.'

'Elizabeth?'

'He did kiss her tonight.'

He would not have believed his grin could get wider or his heart expand more than it did, but… Phillip kissed Elizabeth!

'I feel as though I'm sitting smack in the middle of a miracle,' he confessed. Which was a far cry from where he had been sitting a few moments ago.

'I love you, Ginny.' He placed his arm about her shoulder, drew her close, then rested his chin on top of her head. 'You can't know how much.'

'Perhaps you can prove it to me.' She snuggled against his side, feeling well beyond wonderful.

'I will not compromise you. When you marry me, it will be by your own choice and not because I took advantage.'

'My goodness, Will, I did not expect you would. What I meant is you can prove it by marrying me.'

He kissed her nose, nuzzling it with his larger one.

'Are you set on a large wedding? One with hundreds of flowers and guests? With an orchestra and…never mind. We will not have dancing.'

'I am set for Gretna Green.' And the sooner

the better because she was rather eager to be compromised…within the bonds of marriage. Which would not compromise them, rather be the delightful fulfilment of vows of commitment to each other. 'Think of it! We ran off together before…it would be grandly romantic to do it again.'

'It would be, but there is the matter of a license. We will need one.'

Oh, she had become so caught up in the wonder of it all that she had overlooked the legal aspect of it.

'At first light we shall set out for home to obtain one, rain or shine.'

'It seems we must, but I do not like even a little delay. Each moment will seem like a year.'

He stood and then drew her up with him. 'I did propose to you already, but I would like to do so again.'

'A girl can never have too many.' Especially if offered by the most handsome and bold man she had ever loved…which as it happened was the only man she had ever loved.

He went down on one knee, took her hand in his, then clasped his other hand over his heart.

'Now that I have found you again, Ginny, will you marry me?'

'A hundred times over.' Now she was the one feeling as if she were in the middle of a miracle.

'Once will do.' He stood and gave her a thoroughly delicious kiss. 'But I will love you a hundred times over, every day of my life.'

And that would do nicely as well.

For the rest of the night they sat beside the fire, the cave as cosy a place as she had ever been.

They watched the rain beat down, the lightning strike and the wind blow like a fury.

She was not a bit frightened. Like so many years ago, being with Will made everything all right.

They did not waste time sleeping. There was far too much to talk about. The years that had come between them…the years that lay ahead.

In the middle of a miracle was exactly where they were.

When morning came so did sunshine. Dawn light poked bright fingers inside the cave.

Will released her to stand and stretch. This was the first time they had let go of one another all night.

'There's a carriage down below. We have been found out.'

'They will not be happy that I snuck away.'

'They will not be, but hopefully our news will be well received.'

'It is a lucky thing we came after you,' Mother declared, hurrying towards him and checking him over for any damage he might have suffered in last night's storm. 'You are grinning so I imagine you are well enough.'

'Better than well, Mother.'

He would need to deliver the news of his betrothal and imminent marriage. She might not be best pleased with him for snatching her chosen lady away from Phillip. But at the end of it Mother would have her family united with Aunt Adelia's.

Also, it was not as if Phillip was left heartbroken. He wondered if Mother knew about Elizabeth. If she did, how did she feel about her son's choice?

Glancing towards the stream where the team was tethered, he saw Phillip and Ginny laughing together.

It warmed him, knowing that they would have

the same close relationship that he and Cora had shared.

Life was going to be good…the family healed. Now he only needed to inform his mother of it.

He opened his mouth, but she held up her hand to stop him.

'William, can you forgive me?'

'Have you done something wicked? But don't worry, you are my mother, so you know I will before you ask.'

'Having spent the night in the carriage with your brother…well, let us say he pointed out my mistake in long and drawn-out detail. But Aunt Adelia was as guilty of it as I was.'

'But why were you in the carriage? You have guests…did you really desert them with the ball still going?'

'It was nearly over. But guests do not matter a great deal when one son has run off to sea, when Ginny has commandeered a horse to go after him in a storm and the other son is in a fever to go after you both.'

'It ought to be interesting when everyone finds us all gone.'

'More interesting when they discover your

brother has asked Elizabeth to oversee bidding the guests goodbye.'

'That ought to raise a few brows.' It nearly raised his brows since no announcement of Phillip's intentions had been made. 'Mother, there is something I need to tell you.'

'I imagine so.' He was relieved to see her smiling. The news might not come as such a shock.

'Ginny and I are getting married as soon as we can obtain a special license.'

The carriage door opened. Bishop Stevens stepped out.

'As luck would have it, I have brought one with me.'

'You have a special license?'

'With you?' Ginny asked appearing at his elbow.

'I would hardly allow you to risk living in sin, now would I?'

'I would never—'

'I have known you all your life William. We will ride for Gretna Green with all haste.'

'What good fortune I thought to bring along your wedding gown!' His mother clapped her hands.

'I do not have a wedding gown, Lady Hawk-wood.'

'But of course you do, my dear. Your aunt and I had one made for you weeks ago. It is from Paris and just the loveliest thing. I'm sure you will adore it.'

'We must be on our way if we are to make Gretna Green by tonight. The roads are muddy,' Bishop Stevens pointed out.

'Ginny, my dear girl,' he heard his mother say before he and the Bishop went to join Phillip and help remove brush near the road to clear a path. 'I have asked my sons' forgiveness and now...'

He did not hear the rest, but knew Mother need not worry.

His fiancée was the best, most loving woman imaginable.

William was glad Ginny refused Mother's invitation to ride in the carriage. He wanted her with him...in front of him sharing a horse. They might have each ridden a horse but after believing he had no future with her and now to find he did—and that they would be married tonight—he could not let go of her.

With the extra horse tied behind the carriage, they set off.

Hugging her to his heart with one arm around her ribs, he led the horse around the fallen log. Giving the log a good long glance as they passed by it, he wondered…

'I saw it get hit…watched it split and then fall on the road.'

She nuzzled her head back against his shoulder. He kissed her hair. He thought he would never get enough of kissing her…one lifetime did not contain enough years to get it done.

'It must have been a frightening sight.' He felt a shiver run up her back. How many more hours until he could make her shiver in a different way?

'I wondered if it was a sign…from God. I thought He might be telling me I had made a mistake…that I ought not go to sea…but turn around and confess how I felt about you.'

'That is curious, isn't it? It is where I was when I spotted your fire in the cave. Perhaps the lightning strike was a message.' She sighed. He felt the rise of her breathing slide on his chest. 'I could ride like this for ever, Will…if our wedding wasn't waiting to happen. Can't you urge this horse to pick up his step?'

'I could, but we would not want to tire the poor

beast. What do you say we simply enjoy the moment? Life will happen as it will, but just for now it's you and me…sitting close I can whisper I love you, tickle your ear with it whenever I wish to.'

Like right now. He was rewarded by her quiet laugh.

Behind them he heard the creak of the coach following, the vague conversation of the drivers.

'You don't mind not being Countess?' he asked after a moment.

'Countess? You know I would never want it. But living here? With you?' She swept her hand to take in the fells and the green pastures dotted with grazing sheep. 'Oh, Will, I cannot think of anything more wonderful. And, as if it were not already too good to be believed with my sister living in Windemere, we can raise our children together.'

Children? One could not think of them without thinking of a wedding night…of a lifetime of nights after that…loving, sultry nights as lovers.

Chapter Fifteen

Ginny did have to admit that her wedding gown was exceptional, far too lovely to recite her vows in front of the blacksmith's anvil.

Luckily, she would not need to, not with having Bishop Stevens to do the honours. Given how very thankful she was, it was fitting to recite her vows in front of a man of God.

Now, here she stood in the charming dining room of the inn where they had rented rooms. They were lucky to have three rooms, the owner of the inn told them. They were quite busy and they had got the last of them.

Given that she and Will had been pointed the way by a lightning strike, the message that they were meant for each other given by way of a felled tree, she was more than grateful to be wed properly, pledging her troth before a minister who was also a family friend.

What a complete and utter blessing.

She had only one regret—Aunt Adelia was not here to share her joy. Phillip had searched for her before leaving, but with no luck. Ginny only hoped her aunt would not be distraught when she discovered what she had missed. Knowing her aunt she would not be, rather she would be thrilled by the romance of it all.

Somehow, William had managed to get an expertly tailored wedding suit and he looked dashing in it.

Now, here they stood, vowing to love each other for ever. She could not imagine how a grand cathedral in London would make her any happier than she was in the moment.

Not only happy…but as sparkling as her wedding gown…as light as the evening breeze coming in the open window…as cherished as her groom's gaze upon her said she was as they were pronounced man and wife.

Virginia Penneyjons was now Virginia Talton.

She was his. Even after the words were spoken he could scarcely believe she was his wife. She was his beloved, his Ginny. And she was hungry.

So was he, but in a decidedly different way.

Food was the last thing he had an appetite for. If he had it his way, they would have skipped the meal, gone straight upstairs where he could continue making her his wife.

But Mother had insisted on a celebratory dinner and Phillip arranged it, probably paying a high price to make sure they had the dining room to themselves.

The five of them sat at a table bedecked with a lace cloth and crystal goblets which reflected the amber glow of candlelight.

The food was no doubt excellent, but he ate too quickly to notice. Too bad everyone else was lingering over each bite, talking of this and laughing over that.

As would be expected, there were toasts to be made. Cheers to the bride, to the groom and to the new family now sharing their first meal together.

And a prayer by the Bishop to bless their future as man and wife.

The dining room doors had been left open because the night was uncommonly pretty, with a big bright moon and millions upon billions of stars winking in the sky.

Mother suddenly put down her wine glass. 'What a day! I'm for my bed.'

'I will take a walk under the stars,' Bishop Steven said.

'I'll walk you up, Mother,' Phillip declared with a smile at Ginny and a wink at William.

Halfway across the dining room, his brother turned around. 'I wish you both all the joy I found in my marriage.'

And then he and Ginny were alone for the first time in their married life. The thought of being alone with her whenever he wished made his nerves as jumpy as water dropped in hot grease.

'Come along, my wife. I hope you have eaten your fill.'

'If you are speaking of food, yes, I have.' Standing, she laughed.

He bolted up from his chair because he had never seen her look at him with quite that sort of smile before. Snatching her hand, he raced with her out of the dining room.

The fellow attending the bell desk did not look up. As this was Gretna Green this sort of display of eagerness must be commonplace. For William it was a once-in-a-lifetime event.

At the foot of the stairway, he scooped his bride into his arms, carried her up the stairs and to the end of the hallway where their bridal chamber awaited.

Closing the door, he leaned against it, grinning.

'This time last night I was watching you dance with my brother.'

'This time last night I was certain I would fall on my face.'

What a difference a day could make in one's life. Right now, his primary worry was one of a pleasant nature.

'Tonight, I'm hoping I know how to get that gown off you.'

'It was rather complicated going on, but between us I think we can manage.'

He walked to the window to draw the curtains closed. They were slightly sheer so moonlight lent a pretty glow to the room. He set the bedside lamp to low which gave the chamber an aura of enchantment.

Then again, such enchantment more likely came from a pair of newlyweds in love.

Ginny stood in the centre of a round, blue

rug with white flowers woven at the border. He walked around her in a slow, considering circle, wondering what to unfasten first.

There was a ribbon tied at her neckline in a sweet bow. A likely place to begin. It would give him a chance to stroke the strand of soft hair fallen from her hairdo and grazing her neck.

With a tug, he drew the bow free.

Nothing happened. The gown held steadfastly, encasing his bride in satin and lace.

'I could summon your mother before she falls asleep. She is the one who got me into it.'

'I would rip it off you first.'

'Well, you can't… I'm to have my portrait painted while wearing it.'

'Ah, well, don't worry, Wife… I'm a resourceful fellow and I did learn something about knots when I was at sea.'

'I think there is a knot. It's underneath the skirt…right here near my…oh, well, it's…'

'I'll find it.' He went down on his knees, popped his head under the skirt only to encounter more lace petticoats than would fill a trunk.

They smelled good, though, a bit like roses.

Ah, but then he touched something warm…

firm, no rose petal, but tender flesh. Ginny giggled when he traced his fingers over the spot.

'I'm ticklish behind the knee.'

'Where else?'

'I'm not sure. I imagine we will find out once I'm free of this gown.'

He found a ribbon, among the layers of lace and gave it a tug.

The stiff framework of the bustle sagged.

'There is hope, yet!' he declared, his voice muffled.

He laughed, feeling somewhat victorious over the garment.

Ginny laughed with him.

This was who they were…had always been, loving and laughing.

When he pinched her lightly, higher up, she spun about, freeing his face of froth.

'Cut it?' he asked.

'No.'

He returned his attention to freeing his bride. Ah! He spotted an important-looking button.

'I've wondered about something, Ginny, ever since we've been married.'

'All three hours, you mean?'

He nodded. 'How does anyone get so fortunate as to wed their closest friend? Look, that button did do something.'

But not enough. The gown was still solidly in place. Whoever designed it must not have had a romantic soul.

'There are a few small buttons inside here where you can't see them...' she said while tugging at the bodice of the gown and peering down. 'I don't know how we got so lucky, Will. But I'm so madly grateful for it.'

'So am I. Every morning before I get out of bed, I'm going to take a moment and give thanks for it. Here, I can get them if I feel my way.'

And so that was how it went, he felt his way, slowly and deliciously, plucking this and stroking that until the gown was a puddle around her ankles.

'Happy wedding night, Wife,' he murmured into her ear, his heart as much a puddle as the gown he was stepping on.

With his bride now unencumbered, he carried her slowly towards the bed, kissing her all along the way.

Gratitude did not begin to describe how he

felt in that moment…would feel for the rest of his life.

Ginny had tried to wish Will a happy wedding night, too, but as it turned out, he kept her mouth busy doing other things. Very lovely things that whispered gossip by curious debutantes did not do justice to.

Will had kept his promise to change her from Lady Ginny to Lady Virginia Talton in a more delightful way than she could have imagined. Some changes in life were difficult, this was not one of them. The forging of their marriage bond had been steamy, unrestrained, yet tender. Exquisite was what it was.

Easing up on her side, she studied her new husband's face while he slept.

For as long as she had known him, she had never seen him sleeping. She wanted to touch his long lashes where they curled up at the tip, but she did not wish to wake him.

He had to be exhausted after everything. So, no, she would not touch his lashes, nor would she whisk away the hank of hair that crossed his brow. She would certainly not trace her finger along the crease of his dimple which was present even when he was at rest.

What a marvellous thing it was to be married. Life was not what it had been a day ago.

Then, they had declared their love for each other and it had been beyond incredible.

But vows given to one another and in turn to the Good Lord…then their bodies given to each other… Marriage was vastly different from being in love.

From now on they belonged together. No matter what came they were Mr and Lady Virginia Talton…a set, a pair, meant to see to each other's well-being for the rest of their lives.

How amazing.

Looking back on it, Phillip must have thought her to be silly…asking him to kiss her the way she had. Luckily, her brother-in-law understood what marriage was supposed to be and recognised that he did not have that in his heart for her.

Hmm. Exactly how long did her groom intend to sleep?

Well then, she would touch the curl of his lash and brush back the lock of his hair.

He smiled, then, without opening his eyes,

wrapped his great strong arms around her and rolled her beneath him.

'I love you, Ginny.'

And so he did, until the first rays of dawn stole in the window.

And then they slept…together.

'I hope we are really married. We have no rings on our fingers,' Ginny pointed out, glancing over her shoulder at Will while he buttoned up the back of her gown.

'Good and married,' he answered with a pointed glance at the bed.

As soon as he secured the final button, she turned in his arms and fastened the top button of his shirt.

'It does feel quite a married thing to do to be dressing each other.'

'Undressing even more so,' he pointed out.

She straightened his collar, then observed her handiwork. She had never performed this task before, but she thought she might be gifted at it.

'But think about it, Will…any couple might seek satisfaction for a night and then be gone from each other before sunrise. But to be there in the morning…to be dressing each other? That speaks of commitment.'

'Says to me that the quicker we are dressed and get on with the business of the day, the sooner we will be home…and the sooner I can undress you again.'

'You are very earthy.'

He lifted the hair away from the back of her neck, tickled her with a kiss and then blew warm breath on the spot.

'Like a farmer…or an archaeologist…?' He put his hands at her waist, drawing her tight against his hips. 'Or a groom who cannot get enough of touching his bride.'

'Yes…that last one.'

She was out of breath suddenly and she was certain it was not because of her corset.

'I don't know about you, but I could use a cool walk beside the stream before lunch,' he said.

Yes, a walk would be a good idea.

A short time later they sat beside a stream, their bare feet dangling in cool rushing water.

'Here… I have something I would like to share with you, Will.' She withdrew her journal from a pocket in her skirt, handing it to him.

'Your descriptions of home?'

'I decided to bring it because…well, there is more than landscape on the pages. I feared to leave it unguarded with Lady Della still at the estate.'

'That sounds intriguing.'

'Oh, it is. It's about you…or how I recall you being when you were sixteen years old.' Even though they were married she found she could still blush in front of him, but she did want to share what had been important to her at one time. 'You will see how grateful I was to Lady Kirkwynd for getting it away from Lady Della.'

'I cringe to think about it. We can only hope they are gone when we get home.'

Home. The simple word shot to her heart because it was not at all simple. Home was the place where she and Will would build their lives.

'Lord Handsome and Bold?' His eyes skimmed the pages. What was he thinking? He was smiling…that was something. 'Lady Justina Admirable was exceptionally fond of him…look how she comes to his defence time after time?' He looked up, shot her a grin. 'But you already knew it. I assume you are the admirable lady?'

'I know it sounds silly, Will…it's just that our

day together meant so much to me and this was my way of keeping you in my heart.'

'I like this part where Justina races through a storm…you were brave to do it…to rescue Lord Bold and Handsome from the dark intentions of a…yes, quite clearly it says right here a trollop. But you did come after me in a storm, didn't you?'

Then he started to laugh. What could she do but laugh with him since it was very funny?

'I'm flattered.' He closed the journal, then handed it back to her. 'Truly, Ginny… Justina… thank you for sharing it with me.'

'I had to stop writing about him once I met you. The flesh-and-blood you quite killed him.'

'I must have slayed him with my charm and good looks.'

'You had those aplenty when you were sixteen. What he could not stand up to was your virile, lusty nature.'

His mouth quirked, his brows lowered, exhibiting said virile and lusty nature.

'I wonder how often people walk along the path behind us?' He glanced over his shoulder, looking both ways up and down the path.

'One would be too many for what I am reading in your eyes, Will.'

'Guess we'll have to make use of the water some other way.'

With that he kicked his feet, beating the water and splashing it on them both...which in turn made her laugh while she retaliated with her own kicking.

'Do all couples enjoy playing in water, Will? Or is it just us? Are we peculiar, do you think?'

'We might be, but I would not change it.'

'No, nor me. In fact, I don't think I could live happily ever after with someone who did not laugh at ducks.'

As if saying so summoned them, a family of feathered birds swam past, mama duck quacking, her seven ducklings chirruping.

'If we didn't need to visit the jeweller before we leave Gretna Green, I'd scoop them up and give them to you as a wedding gift.'

What a funny thing to imagine, Will dashing about attempting to capture the quick little creatures while their mother quacked up a big fuss.

'Ducks could be a symbol of our love, Will. We shall build a cottage of our own and call it "Duckies Den".'

'For now, what do you say we put on our shoes and go to the jeweller? I'd like to give you a symbol of my love and fidelity with something more durable than feathers.'

'Feathers are durable…but gold sparkles,' she pointed out while they approached the jeweller's closed door.

'Feathers do sparkle, when they are in sunlight,' he said while opening the door to the shop. 'It's only fair to say so. But gold it is…and a diamond or—'

'Aunt Adelia!' Ginny cried out because there she was, bent at the waist and peering into the glass jewellery case with Lord Helm beside her.

Curiously close beside her.

Dashing forward, she caught her aunt up in a hug. 'I can't believe you are here.'

'Oh…but there is not a nicer place to be wed than Gretna Green, is there, now?'

'Not if one wishes to wed quickly…and I cannot understand why anyone would care to wait months and months.'

'It is a relief to hear you say so, my dear.' Aunt Adelia's smile was blushing pink and joyful.

Ginny felt Will smiling. Even though she was not touching him or even looking at him, she sensed it was what he was doing. It must have to do with being married...newlywed intuition.

'I tried to find you, Auntie, but Will was running away to sea.'

Aunt Adelia looked confused for a moment. And why not? What she said made little sense without knowing the rest of it.

'I'm sorry,' Aunt Adelia said. 'I should have told you where I was going...but when the idea overtook us...well, we were rather helpless to do anything else.'

Ginny backed out of the hug...so did Aunt Adelia.

Clasping hands, they stared at one another.

'But, Aunt Adelia, if you left before I did, how did you know I had even gone? Let alone where to find me?'

'Ginny...' Will leaned close to her ear and spoke quietly. 'I do not think she found us. We found her...and Lord Helm.'

'Not find us? But here she is... Good afternoon, Lord Helm.'

'Lord Helm,' Will said. 'Would you and Lady Helm care to have lunch with us?'

What! Lady Helm?

'Auntie! You got married?'

'It appears that Bishop Stevens was busy giving out special licenses,' William said.

'But how did you know where to find us? The Bishop said he would keep our secret.'

'He did manage to keep it… I came here to be married, too! And I am!'

They leapt back into a hug, rocking each other for a moment. 'But where is dear Phillip.'

'Phillip?'

She glanced at Will.

'Oh… I see.' Auntie tapped her chin, smiling, laughing with her eyes. 'You chose the tingle after all.'

'Well, Auntie, it was very hard to ignore.'

'Congratulations to you both,' Lord Helm declared, grinning and pumping Will's hand up and down vigorously. 'Thank you for your offer of lunch. I, for one, am famished.'

'We'll be along after we have solidified our vows with rings,' Ginny said.

'While that is lovely, it is clear to see that your vows have already been solidified quite acceptably,' Auntie answered with a wink.

Two hours later, with rings on their fingers and lunch finished, they were on the road home.

It was lovely and private in the carriage. Mother, Phillip, and the Bishop rode with the newly wedded Lord and Lady Helm, the spare horses tied to the back of the carriage.

'I still cannot believe my aunt ran off and got married at her age. Can you, Will?'

'I can.' How she adored his smile. She would never get tired of seeing it. 'Shall I show you why?'

He touched her chin, turning her face so that her lips were only inches from his.

And then he kissed her, reminding her that they were alone in the carriage and would be for hours…just them, Mr and Lady Virginia Talton with a long journey ahead. Hours in which they could indulge in whatever way they wished to pass the time.

Well then, the thought made her hot and bothered, as if her clothes were too tight.

She felt his breath skim over her lips when he whispered, 'Did you feel that?'

'It was hard to miss, you do kiss rather well.'

'Apparently so does Lord Helm. Ginny, the tingle does not go away…age has nothing to do with love. I find that excellent news.'

'Oh, the best…we shall do our utmost to keep the tingle tingling.'

'Practice makes perfect,' he murmured.

He murmured it while he was kissing her. How did he manage it?

Well, she had the rest of her life to find out.

The library at Hawkwood—two years later

My dearest, far oldest and most dependable friend Adelia,

You and your husband must come with all haste. The estate is overrun with infants.

Ginny and William's twins have begun to walk. They toddle about, putting themselves at risk with every step. Even though they tumble down with every other step, I cannot keep up with them on my own. And Ginny certainly cannot, being so near the end of her term.

Would you believe she is trying to complete furnishing Duckies' Den? Oh, yes, they did give the cottage that odd name. Perhaps they wish to keep visitors away.

Be that as it may, I need you here. I dreamed that you dreamed she gave birth to another set of twins…two more boys! I urge

you, beg you, as only a friend for as long as we have been can ask, pack your bags and come to Hawkwood without delay.
Devotedly, your dearest, oldest and most weary friend,
Violet

The writing desk of Lady Helm—one day later

My dearest, extraordinarily oldest and quite lucky friend Violet,
My bags were packed before your letter reached me. I did indeed have a dream. But you were wrong about Ginny again having twin boys...no, indeed, this time she will have twin girls...and, oh, but they will be quite the loveliest and feistiest babies. We shall have great fun.

But get what rest you can, my dear, because that was not the whole of the dream. It gets even more delightful. Phillip and Elizabeth will return from London with happy news of their own...and a pair of large puppies who like nothing more than to chew.

Expect me and Lord Helm within days. I can scarce believe how well our plans have borne fruit. Get the flutes ready to be filled

with champagne. We shall toast to an ever-growing number of small feet pattering about!
With joyful regards,
Your oldest and most joyful friend,
Adelia

* * * * *

LET'S TALK

Romance

For exclusive extracts, competitions
and special offers, find us online:

f facebook.com/millsandboon

⊙ @millsandboonuk

🐦 @millsandboon

Or get in touch on 0844 844 1351*

For all the latest titles coming soon,
visit millsandboon.co.uk/nextmonth

*Calls cost 7p per minute plus your phone company's price per
minute access charge

Want even more
ROMANCE?

Join our bookclub today!

'Mills & Boon books, the perfect way to escape for an hour or so.'

Miss W. Dyer

'Excellent service, promptly delivered and very good subscription choices.'

Miss A. Pearson

'You get fantastic special offers and the chance to get books before they hit the shops'

Mrs V. Hall

Visit millsandbook.co.uk/Bookclub and save on brand new books.

MILLS & BOON

Carol Arens delights in tossing fictional characters into hot water, watching them steam, and then giving them a happily-ever-after. When she's not writing she enjoys spending time with her family, beach-camping or lounging about in a mountain cabin. At home, she enjoys playing with her grandchildren and gardening. During rare spare moments you will find her snuggled up with a good book. Carol enjoys hearing from readers at carolarens@yahoo.com or on Facebook.